*The man
behind the goal*

The man
behind the goal

and other short stories

Brian Glanville

First published in 2015 by WSC Books Ltd
Studio 202, 7 Whitechapel Road, London E1 1DU
www.wsc.co.uk
info@wsc.co.uk

ISBN 978-0-9561011-4-3

Compiled and edited by Brian Glanville, Andy Lyons, Tom Hocking and Richard Guy
Cover design by Doug Cheeseman
Cover photos by Paul Thompson / WSC Photography
Printed in the UK by CPI Group UK, Croydon CR0 4YY

Contents

Introduction

I met Brian Glanville for the first time in the Stade Gerland, Lyon, the 1998 World Cup, Group E. Mexico were playing South Korea, a game now remembered – if at all – for Cuauhtémoc Blanco's froggy hop. The match was of little significance to England and there were few British journalists in attendance. FIFA placed the small band together, so that our fierce inquiries of 'Who put in the cross they just scored from?' would find an answer, even if it wasn't the correct one.

Brian appeared at the top of the stairs wearing a tan mac and carrying a portable Olivetti typewriter in a sky-blue case. As he walked down the steps he called out salutations in a variety of languages, and responded in kind to the foul-mouthed greetings of his compatriots.

He had been allocated the seat next to mine, flopped down into it and, surveying the field on which the two sides had lined up for the national anthems, commented, 'As Porfirio Déaz remarked, "Poor Mexico, ¡*Tan lejos de Dios y tan cerca de los Estados Unidos!*"'

If I had ever pictured my first encounter with one of the legends of British football writing I guess I might have hoped for a scene like this one.

At the age of ten, when it slowly dawned on me that I was not going to be the next George Best, I conceived an idea of becoming a sports journalist (Ah, the crazy dreams of children). I drew my inspiration from newspapers, magazines and books: Hugh McIlvanney, Frank Keating, the Australian cricket writer Ray Robinson and George Plimpton, whose account of a spell training with the Detroit Lions my father had picked up at the bookstore in Rome airport on his way back from visiting a blast furnace in Apulia. Brian Glanville was high on that list, not so much for the pieces he wrote in the *Sunday Times*, or his definitive history of the World Cup, but for his fiction. In my primary school library were two books more well-thumbed than most: Bill Naughton's *The Goalkeeper's Revenge* and Glanville's *Goalkeepers Are Different*, with its green and blue action cover.

Later I'd read Brian Glanville's other football fiction, borrowing it from the village library when I was old enough to venture into the grown-ups' section. Both *The Rise of Gerry Logan* (spoken of in glowing terms by Franz Beckenbauer) and *The Dying of the Light* I last read when I was 14 or 15. The plots and characters I no longer recall, what remains is a powerful sense of atmosphere: post-match dressing rooms filled with sullen rage, the bitter odour of sweat and embrocation, the clatter of studs on wet tiles, the ache of old bruises pressed again.

I encountered it once more reading the stories in this collection. Most are set in the Britain of my childhood, a slightly seedy place of mist and dampness, the smell of boiled cabbage and throat lozenges, of greasy hair inadequately covering a widening bald spot.

Football, it goes without saying, was different then. This is a world of players named Jimmy and Ron, tough cup ties at Preston, £7,000 transfer fees, agents living above suburban sweetshops, wild nights of light ale and 'crumpet' that end when the pubs shut at 11. It is all beautifully evoked; the pressmen in their shapeless raincoats and 'saucerless cups of undrinkable tea' hoping for 'the occasional prize of a small cake', the chairman 'who has about him the prosaic, suspicious air of a successful grocer'.

It's done with compassion, too. There is no sneering here at the aspirations of working-class men, or the irrational dreams of hangers on and would be coaches. The twist in the stories often comes through a shift in empathy. Sympathy is with the losers, however ill-suited for it they may at first appear.

Not all the stories are set in England. Some of the best take place in Italy, a country which, back then, contrasted more sharply with Britain than it does today (my first visit to Rome as a 15-year-old was like going from black-and-white television straight into widescreen Technicolor). Here is sunshine and vivid glamour, big money, and suave fixers manoeuvring with an 'air of constant conspiracy', not so much – you suspect – from necessity as because they enjoy everything much more that way.

My favourite, *The Prodigy*, centres on a Tuscan boy, Piero Avanzolini, whose father has trained him since childhood to make him a top-class player. (The notion of a perfect scientific coaching formula features in a few of the stories. It was a mad fixation of the era. Nowadays we have stats-fed Moneyball instead.) The father is a Fascist journalist who stalks the touch-lines while his son is playing, 'a trail of cigarette butts marking his progress'.

The Prodigy and the other stories in this collection have been out of print for some while. I am glad they are back. Football has been far too poorly served by fiction writers to allow such good work to languish.

Harry Pearson

The man behind the goal

He had brought his own football. It lay on the ground beside the bench, where he himself sprawled in clumsy comfort, his head pillowed on his hands, his heavy, muddy boots propped against the wooden arm. The bench stood beside some railings, at the foot of a little slope of leafless trees. The park had gone from autumn into winter; puddles lay, blind and brown, in the declivities of the little football field; raindrops hung from the white crossbars of the goals.

I did not greet the man when I arrived; my first reaction was to resent him. He was filling up the bench where we always changed, his boots had fouled it with pats of mud, and – supine and unembarrassed – he gave no sign of moving.

"It'll rain again," he announced, in an accent I could not quite place. "See the clouds up there? Black ones. It'll pour." I nodded, and began to take off my tracksuit. In a moment, I looked up and saw Don coming down the hill that led from the road, his fair, bushy head bowed; unseeing, or not wanting to see: I was never sure. His leather bag swung from his hand.

The man did not speak to me again; he seemed perfectly relaxed. From a haversack beside him, he took out an apple and raising his head like a fish rising to a bait, began to eat it, in noisy bites.

Don was beside us now. We looked at the man, exchanged shrugs and glances, and hung our clothes over the spiked fence. Don took a football out of his case and rolled it on to the ground.

"Hard, is it?" asked the man, casting a sidelong glance. "Yes, it looks hard. Mine's soft, soft as bloody putty. Useless. Can't get nobody to blow it up."

Then, as though his attention could be switched on and off like an electric current, he went back to his apple as though he had never spoken, and finally, with a contemptuous flick of the hand, his eyes still fixed on the sky, he threw the core over the fence.

Don and I moved on to the football pitch, and he went into goal; the goal beneath the great, chimneyed monolith of the power station. I shot, the ball rose high over the crossbar, and Don turned to trot after it, a patient and unhurried sheep dog. Out of the corner of an eye, I saw the little man had got off the bench, and was playing with his own football, a small, stooping, under-nourished figure in a blue boiler suit, gambolling about the ball, half gnome, half puppy, head bent over it, in earnest concentration. In his fantasy, he was clearly a forward, tricking and bewildering a host of defenders, now skipping over the ball, now pulling it to him with the sole of his foot, now feinting to his left, and stroking it to the right. From a distance, the ball invisible, it must have seemed like a grotesque ritual dance, a leprechaun frolicking round his crock of gold.

There was a thump and a splash, as our football landed beside me in a puddle; as I turned to get it, the little man suddenly whirled, to kick his ball under the seat – obviously he'd scored a goal. I shot again, looked round again, and now the little man had recovered his ball and was dribbling it towards us over the bumpy ground, with the same dedication, the same ungainly diligence. I wondered for a moment if he meant to join us, but he made no effort to come on to the pitch, merely dribbling the ball on and on, head bent, until he was behind our goal.

Again I shot. This time the ball sailed between the netless goalposts, high past Don's outstretched right arm; and at this the little man turned from his own soft ball and scampered after ours, catching it, turning on it with a short, self-conscious pirouette, as though he were demonstrating to a class, then, with the same, studied technique, he kicked it back to us.

I shouted thanks, feeling a stab of guilt, sorry I had dealt so brusquely with him. I half hoped that he would go away or, if he stayed, concentrate upon his own strange, intense gyrations. But each time the ball flew behind the goal, he was after it like a faithful bird dog, dribbling it back with his painful, stooping run, until at last, with a kick laboured but accurate, he would send it back on to the pitch. "Thank you!" we called, "thank you! thank you!" But we were still uneasy; he had placed us in his debt.

We trained once a week, and we thought we had seen the last of him, but he was there again the following Thursday, boots up on the bench, his half-pumped pudding of a ball beside it. Again, he trotted behind the goal when we began to shoot, again he endlessly chased the ball and sent it back to us, but now he maintained a ceaseless and staccato commentary.

"On the ground... keep it on the *ground*... if you put it in the air, you've lost it, you're wasting it!" A breathless dash to retrieve the ball. "The *Scottish* way's the best... I don't mean the new way, because that's rubbish; I mean the old way, the classical way." Another dash. "I told them at Tottenham, I was on the terrace… Spurs? I said… Great *team*, I said? They're not fit to lace the boots… up in the air, the whole time… that big Smith; the other big one, Norman… Up in the air, biff and bang … I *told* them, that's not football. Football is on the *ground*."

I still could not locate his accent, that now, in its harsh fluency, seemed Welsh, now from the North East. When we left the field, he trotted beside us, still urging and admonishing, while we listened with half an ear, responding now and then in monosyllables. Close at hand, he cut an oddly contradictory figure, half boy, half man: boyish in his slim fragility, the clear, washed grey of his eyes, the straight hair dangling, like a boy's, over his forehead; unboyish in the greyness of that hair, the waxy yellow of his sunken cheeks. At moments, I would look at him and think of an old man; at others, almost of a child; but in his humped, compulsive movements, there was nothing child-like. I thought of him as some poor, harmless paranoid; a garrulous tramp with a strange obsession, who probably slept rough, out in the park; a cliché figure made over-familiar by playwrights of the avant garde; life imitating art.

He needed a disciple, that was obvious, and he must have known that we – casual, mediocre Sunday footballers – were too old and frivolous for his purpose. But the next week, when we arrived in the rain, the pupil had been found; a sturdy, stupid boy who stood ox-like under the downpour, woodenly watching, as the little man pirouetted round the soggy ball. "He'll get pneumonia," I said, and wondered at his toughness, his fanaticism. He was too frail to spurn the weather.

When Don and I reached the goal behind which he was standing – this time the upper goal – we could hear him instructing the boy with the same, hortatory voice, as though he were addressing a youth rally. "If you come *over* ball like this!" – a skip and a jump – "it is useless. What you *want* to do is to approach it like *this*, then you take it way like *that*, thus leaving your opponent in two minds."

The boy nodded his heavy pink cheeked head, he was not invited to try himself.

"More *haste*, less *speed*; it's the same thing with your kicking. With the instep. The toe of the boot *down* – like this. And *then*, the follow-through – like *that!*" The ball merely skidded across the muddy ground, but the boy did not laugh: nor did he fetch it. Instead, the little man set off after the ball, with his familiar, crab-like run, caught it, dribbled back and cried, "I shall now demonstrate the pass with the inside of the foot!"

It was raining more heavily than ever. The boy's coarse, black hair was soaked; raindrops ran down his plump cheeks, but still he stood, impassive. It was twenty minutes before he left, plodding his stolid, unathletic way across the wet grass, to disappear at last over the hill. The little man resumed his old position behind the goal, and now it was us whom he exhorted.

"Too high, too high! I was telling that boy: *always* along the ground! Keep it down, and you'll go *up*! Keep it up, and you'll go *down*!" The slippery ball made his kicking more feeble and erratic than ever, and he began to complain. "It's my boots are the trouble! If *I* could get these boots right! I can't kick with these. It's no use trying." Back and forth he ran, under the teeming rain, fetching and kicking, fetching and kicking. His hair, plastered damply to his forehead, gave him more than ever the appearance of a tonsured monk: I could see him in a brown cassock, hobbling after the ball as he hobbled now.

"If *I* had my boots, right. If *I* could only get some boots!"

The next time we trained, I brought him an old pair of shoes. I put them underneath the bench – clotted with mud, strewn with newspapers and ravaged brown parcels – while he pursued his ball, on the football pitch. I did not mention the shoes – somehow the gesture reeked of charity, a need for gratitude – nor did he himself ever allude to them! But he had them on his feet, the following Thursday.

I came upon him unawares that day, though at first I thought he knew I was there. He was talking in a loud, cheerful voice I had not heard before smiling, stretched full length, again, on the seat. He was reading the *Daily Express*, and I saw, with some surprise, that it was the latest.

"You read these things," he was saying, "and what do they expect you to believe? Three quarters of its lies, lies for gullible people. President Eisenhower accuses Kruschev. If you bought the *Daily Worker*, it would say, President Kruschev accuses Eisenhower. Which of them is true? Probably neither! I don't bloody well believe one nor the other."

I greeted him: "Reading the paper?"

He tilted back his head, grinning at me. "I was engaged in listening to the finest music in the world; the sound of my own voice." Suddenly I liked him better. For the first time, the harsh, hectoring tone had gone; the eyes, more palely luminous than ever, were full of a humour at once subversive and self-deprecating.

"You're here every day?" I asked.

"Every day, rain or shine, wind or weather, hell or high water."

"And... do you camp here?"

"No," he said, contemptuously. "I live down in Westminster, at the Salvation Army hostel – if you can call it living. What they give you to eat, you couldn't feel a sparrow on. One rotten little sausage for breakfast, a few mouldy baked beans at night. If I didn't go out and buy my own bread, I'd starve." He gestured, and I sat beside him, half hidden by his body, a brown loaf, crudely hacked by the penknife that lay beside it. "Here every day," he said, "I never get bored, listening to myself. Out in the fresh air. Sometimes I have arguments; it's a way to pass the time. Other times I recite poetry."

"Which poetry do you prefer?" "My own!" he said, and gave the same mischievous smile. "They talk about great poetry.

"In Xanadu did Kubla Khan

"A stately pleasure dome decree.

"Dee–dum, dee–dum, dee–dum, dee–dum,

"Dee–dum, dee–dum, dee–dum, dee–dee."

"Call that poetry? I don't call it poetry."

It was a chance to ask him where he came from.

"Northumberland," he said – as I had half suspected. "A little village up there. Don't ask me what it's like now, I haven't been back there for 35 years. I never wanted to. I've been all over the world – India, France, Italy, Spain. Why should I go back to a village in Northumberland? I never liked it here. If I go anywhere, I'll go to France again."

"What were you doing in France?'

"Learning the language. I was there a year ago, I was in Marseilles. When I think I'll go to a place, nobody stops me; I make up my mind, and then I go."

"And India?'

"I was in the army, I was there till 1939, when the war came. Then I told them I was ill; my stomach, I said. Fifteen doctors looked at me, they had me in three different hospitals, but they couldn't get to the bottom of it, none of them could. They had to discharge me. Because I hadn't joined the army to fight a war, I'd joined the army in peacetime."

"Is the boy coming today? Your pupil ?" "Oh, him," he said, "he'll be here later. I'll make a footballer out of him. I've told him 'I'll make you one, if it kills me. I'll make you one if it kills us both.' I've got the perfect system, see. I have devised this system lying here and thinking; it is a triumph of mind over matter." The hortatory voice was coming back. "*Whereby*, if the material is young enough, *any* player can be turned into a champion. I'm too old, now, or I'd use it on myself."

I looked round; Don was making his steady, long-legged way down the hill. The little man glanced up suddenly at a tree above him and said, "That's another thing I've been thinking about; photosynthesis. They say a tree keeps alive by what it draws into itself through its leaves. Well, how can that tree possibly be alive, then"– and his voice rose as though it were a personal affront – "how can it *possibly* be alive when it hasn't *got* a bloody leaf?"

Looking again at the little man and his pupil, I knew that whatever scheme he had devised, the plump boy would never make a footballer. Indeed, it grew clearer and clearer as one watched that the scheme was an end in itself, the boy no more than a lay-figure, scarcely permitted a kick at the ball, while his master pranced and pirouetted like a lame pit pony.

Indeed, for the boy to be a pupil at all, it was essential that he should be inept; a more proficient boy would never have stood for it.

The following week, I brought the little man a parcel of food; a loaf of bread, a packet of butter, a few tins of soup and spaghetti. From his prone position on the bench, he thanked me seriously.

"I need that, it'll help me, that. The food they give you down there..." He was silent awhile, looking gravely into space. "I have decided," he said, at last, his tone implying lonely hours of contemplation, "that soccer is the finest game of all: because there is nothing *evolutionary* about it. Cricket, croquet, hockey, billiards: they are all evolutionary. They are played with a club. A man with a club in his hand is only one stage further than an ape. Football is a game that Plato would have liked, it might have been invented by the Greeks; I can pay no higher compliment. That was the finest flowering of human civilisation."

Looking at him closely, it seemed to me that his yellow cheeks were hollower than ever. Over his blue dungarees, which conferred on him a spurious dignity of labour, he wore an old khaki greatcoat, but it wasn't enough to sustain his Promethean defiance of the weather.

Again the boy arrived, again the demonstration and the exhortations, though this time, he was allowed to do a little more for himself. He did it clumsily, without confidence or optimism, more, without visible enthusiasm. I wondered if he had simply been accosted while passing by, a wedding guest to the little man's Ancient Mariner, hypnotised first into staying, then into coming back, again and again.

The next week, he was for the first time wearing football shorts, showing his plump, white, heavy thighs, but his movements were as rigid as ever. A fortnight later, when I asked about him, the little man replied," I have decided he is ready. I have decided he is ready to take part in a game, using the principles that I have taught him. On Saturday, he's playing in a trial match for his school. I am going there, and I shall advise him from the touchline."

"Have you seen him play before?"

"Never before; it wasn't necessary. It didn't interest me, because he had not imbibed my principles. But even in these few weeks, he has improved; I can see it for myself, and he's told me that he has: his teachers are amazed. Otherwise he wouldn't have been chosen for this trial."

Suddenly I felt alarm for him. He was trying to impose his fantasy world upon the real, and the consequence could only be failure, disappointment. I could see him wandering up and down the touchline of the football ground, while loutish, spotted schoolboys giggled at him, and their teachers looked at him with outrage. He'd be disillusioned and humiliated; yet how could he be warned?

"Isn't it a bit early?" I asked. "You haven't been teaching him long."

"I have been teaching him three or four times a week, up to two hours, for the last five weeks. That is at least 30 hours. All that is necessary to reach a good standard in boys' football is 30 hours' tuition. To reach the international standard, I have estimated it will take three hundred hours."

For a little while, he kicked our football back for us, from behind the goal; then the boy came lumbering along, for his tuition.

The following week, the little man was not to be seen; indeed, his very bench had gone, and I surmised a conspiracy, a persecution of park-keepers. From time to time, as Don and I trained together, I looked up the hill, or behind me into the green distance of the park, half expecting him to appear; but he did not come. I missed him, wondering if we should ever see him again, whether he'd decamped from the park because the boy had failed, and he could not longer face us, the boy, the workshop of his failure.

A week later, the bench was still not there. We had been running up and down, passing the ball, for several minutes, and were just beginning to take shots at goal, when there was a scampering and a flurry of branches on the hillside beneath which the bench had stood, and the little man emerged, his eyes wide and staring – almost, I thought, like poor, mad Ben Gunn. He was wearing his army greatcoat, which hung nearly to the ground, and I wondered how he would negotiate the railings. But just before he got to them, he pulled himself up, with a quick, monkey-like movement, by the branch of a tree and, from the tree, he dropped over the fence.

He shuffled across the field towards us, and the goal, without taking off the coat. Even before I saw his face, I could tell his dejection by the way he moved. He could never be graceful, but now his old, obsessional vitality had left him, too. He seemed to be carrying out a duty, even – incongruously – a job. He took no notice of our greeting, but went on past us without a word. His face looked sick and ravaged, jaundiced, yellower than ever, crumbling away, like the face of a dying man; the eyes had nothing in them but a blank, possessed determination. He kicked the ball back to us as devotedly as ever, but in silence, without commentary or criticism. The change was such that it depressed us both, so that we finished training early. We thanked the little man, but he turned away without a word, hopelessly, making slowly towards the middle of the park.

I caught up with him. "How did the game go?" I asked.

"Him?" he said, and stopped. "Him? He was useless. I miscalculated. I shall have to go back to the beginning. I had decided that, using my system, any human material could be turned into a successful footballer. Now I can see that I was wrong; there must be basic talent, therefore the system is still not perfect. It may take years to perfect; I don't know if I have enough time left to me." "Of course you have," I said, but the words sounded false, the consolation cheap. He made no answer, turning his back to me, as I felt I deserved, and trudged away again. For a few moments, I was half determined to go after him; then I, too, turned away. He was like a sick dog, wanting to be left alone.

He was not there the next week, or the next and I began to feel anxious for him: he looked in retrospect too much like a wounded animal, crawling off to die. In the third week, I met the boy; he came slowly across the football pitch, while Don and I were tugging off our boots. About him, too, there seemed to be a sadness, something over and above his usual stolidity.

I called to him and, without increasing pace, he came over. "Do you know where he is?" I asked. "The little man."

"I dunno," he said, in the incongruous, piping voice of plump adolescence. "I don't think he's well. He may have gone to hospital."

"Hospital? When did you see him last?""

"About two weeks ago. I wanted him to teach me again, but he wouldn't. He wouldn't speak to me." Aggrieved, the voice rose higher still. "I can't help it if I didn't play well. I couldn't help it if they told him to go away; it wasn't my fault."

"Was he ill, then?" "Yeah, he looked terrible. He said he hadn't eaten for three days. I came back the next day, I brought some apples for him, but he wasn't there. I never seen him again."

That evening, I telephoned the Salvation Army hostel, who identified him without difficulty. Yes, they said, he had gone into hospital; they told me which it was. It was exposure, they thought; they were not quite sure. "Well, I'm not surprised," said the voice, as though I had somehow accused it. "The *weather* he stayed out in."

The following day, I went to the hospital with a paper carrier bag of fruit. I waited on a bench in the dim, bleak entrance hall, among a murmuring, worried crowd of visitors, dragooned and overawed; the poor at the mercy of the hospital. A bell rang and we filed along a twilit corridor. Here and there, we passed the entrance of a ward, where the patients sat up in their beds with taut expectancy. At each of these a few of us would file away, and there would be small cries of joy, embraces.

At last I reached the ward where he was lying, and looked in through the door. It was very long, a row of beds ran down each side. At first I could not see him, but at last I made him out. He sat, motionless and upright, against the pillows, in a bed halfway down the left-hand wall, his face more wasted than ever. But it was not this which shocked me, so much as the expression of the eyes, void now of humour or defiance, merely staring out across the ward.

A nurse came up to me with her brisk, starched walk, and asked whom I wanted to see. I pushed the bag of fruit into her hands and pointed at him, then turned away, fearful he should recognise me.

Nemesis had caught up with him, society and the weather had beaten him at last.

I hurried into the street, escaping with the memory of his courage.

Goalkeepers are crazy

It was no good everyone telling me I was taking a chance, because I knew that better than they did. It stood to reason, anyway; you don't let an international class goalkeeper go for seven thousand quid unless there's something wrong with him, and I reckoned I knew what it was.

The thing was I had to get someone quickly; what with Ron Gavin out for the whole season with a broken leg and Jim Mason copping it the very first game, we were having diabolical bloody luck.

So I signed him. I knew he'd be after something for himself, and so he was at first, but when I told him my club wouldn't have anything to do with that kind of carry-on, he just backed down without a fuss; it surprised me. London did it, I suppose, they all want to come to London, though God knows why; think the streets are paved with gold and crammed with crumpet. Maybe they are, now, but they never were when I was a player; you had to work for anything you got.

"I've got a tart in London," he said, "bloody marvellous, do anything you like, she will," and I thought that's a damn good start, with him married and a kid. The first day he came in for training I had him into my office.

"Look here," I told him, "I know all about you. If you're playing for my club, you're going to behave yourself, otherwise out you go, understand? As far as I'm concerned, you start with a clean sheet, but if you want to stay here, you'll do what you're told and you'll keep out of trouble." He didn't say much, just muttered something about giving a dog a bad name, and seeing him standing there I began to feel a bit sorry for speaking so harsh – though I'd seen him with my own eyes kick our centre-forward, the season before last, and put him out for a fortnight. Still, he looked more sinned against than sinning, a sort of dead end kid with hollow cheeks and shifty eyes that never looked at you; like a dog that's got used to people kicking it and shies away when anyone comes near. Looking at him you'd never think he was a professional footballer at all, let alone a goalkeeper, but I wasn't worried about that side of it. He was good enough for me on the field, so long as he behaved himself off it.

Well he couldn't have started better. The first Saturday he goes out and he plays a blinder. I'm not kidding, there were at least three shots he wasn't entitled to get near, and he not only got to them, he held them.

Then he goes and spoils everything two minutes from the end. He catches the ball, the centre-forward comes in naughty with his foot up, and Wilkins tucks the ball under one arm and takes a ruddy great swing at him. Luckily the referee had seen what happened first, so he let him off with a warning. I didn't say anything about it to him when he came off the field, I just told him he'd done well, but that Monday I had him up to my office and I didn't half pitch into him.

"Look," I said, "what do you want to go and do a silly thing like that for? Where do I stand if you go and get yourself suspended? I have to start looking for a goalkeeper all over again and it can cost me another seven thousand pounds."

"Well," he said, "don't blame me, I was provoked." That was the word: provoked.

"Of course you were provoked," I said, "everybody gets provoked in this game, and if they do what you did every time it happens, you might as well hire Harringay and turn it into a boxing match."

"Well," he said, with his head all on one side in the way he had, "he'd kept threatening me. He said, I'm going to get you, Wilkins." You wouldn't believe it.

"Then the next time it happens," I told him, "tell him you'll get him first. Keep it to words. Words don't hurt anybody."

For the next few games everything went all right, he was still playing well, and I was beginning to think maybe people had been a bit hard on him, that he was all right if only you handled him properly. Then things started to go wrong off the field. The first thing was that I heard he was going round the clubs, and taking some of the younger players with him. I'd noticed he went about with them mostly, although he was older than they were, in fact I was afraid there might be a bit of a clique forming, and I didn't want that if I could help it. Things like that always show on the field – you can't avoid it.

Anyway, I knew what must be happening. You've always got a bunch of spivs hanging round any big London team, cadging tickets off the players to flog on the black market, and getting a cheap thrill out of being seen in their company. I didn't mind the boys selling their complimentaries over the odds to make a bit on the side, it was what it led to that I was scared of. Most of these characters seem to hang round the shady little clubs in Soho, and before you know where you are they've got the lads going there drinking, then fixing themselves up with women, and that's it.

I didn't do anything about it for the moment, I just kept an eye on what was going on to see how far I thought it would lead. Apart from that, Wilkins was playing well and I'd got no complaints about him except that he was a moaner. I've nothing against the Welsh, but it seems to me moaning in a Welsh accent is the worst ruddy moaning of all. Everybody was against him – not only refs and linesmen and reporters and players on the other side, but even waiters and porters and bus conductors. It was incredible. He came to me before one match and said he didn't want to play. "That referee hates me," he said. I couldn't believe my ears.

"Of course he doesn't bloody well hate you," I said. "A referee's a sort of policeman; he's there to keep order on the field. If you get drunk and disorderly and a copper hauls you inside, you don't say he hates you, do you? He's only doing his job." That didn't put a stop to it, though; not a bit of it.

"I tell you he's got it in for me," he says. "He took my name last season against Burnley. And the next time he's refereeing a game of ours, he comes up to me and he says, 'I've got my eye on you, Wilkins. Do one thing wrong and you're off this bloody field'."

"Well," I said, "did he send you off the field?"

"No," he says, "he didn't," almost as though he was disappointed.

"Well, then," I told him, "you haven't got anything to worry about, have you? I know those kind of referees; their bark's always worse than their bite. All you want to do is kid them along – say yes sir, I won't give you anything to worry about. That'll make him feel like a little tin god, and he'll leave you alone for the rest of the game." That should have convinced him if anything could, but I could see I wasn't getting through. He said something I couldn't properly hear about still being sure the bloke had it in for him, and I could see we might be in for trouble. I told Gerry Gray to keep an eye on him from centre-half, to be ready to nip in and grab him if anything seemed to be going wrong.

Well, it did. For twenty minutes everything's going like clockwork, the boys playing well, we're a goal up, and I'm up in the stand and I'm laughing. Then the ball comes through to their centre-forward, who looks as if he's standing a yard offside, he bangs it in, and the referee gives them a goal. Well, Wilkins went mad. I tell you I've never known a player like it; talk about Jekyll and bloody Hyde. Off the field you'd think all he ever wanted was to milk the club for everything he could get; on it, it was like he stood to lose a hundred pounds every time he let in a goal. Before Gerry could get hold of him, he'd raced up to this referee, had him by the shoulder, and practically spun him right round. The bloke had his notebook out in a flash, but it didn't have any effect; it looked for a moment as if the boy was so far gone he was going to hit him – which would have meant suspension sine die. I was up on my feet and I don't mind admitting it, my heart was in my mouth. Then Gerry got to him just in time, grabbed him round the middle, and pulled him away.

For the rest of that game, every time the ball was in our penalty area I could hardly bear to look. It wasn't so much I was afraid they were going to score – it was what Wilkins would do to the referee if they did. Anyway, everything held up till a minute from full time and then the worst thing happens you'd think it was possible to happen. We gave away a penalty. Their centre-forward's right through, and Gerry brings him down flat on his face. I shut my eyes I could just imagine what was going to happen. When I opened them again, though, there was Wilkins standing on his goal line, meek as a bloody lamb. Then they take the kick and what does he do but go and save it. I just sat there and I didn't know whether to laugh or to cry. I was sure of one thing, though; if this sort of caper was going to go on, I'd be up the pole before the end of the season. Maxwell, one of the directors, comes up to me after the match and says, "We've got a good goalkeeper, there, haven't we, Jack? Don't you think he's a good goalkeeper?"

"If you really want to know what I think," I said, "I think he's a bloody madman."

"Oh, I wouldn't say that, Jack," he says, "I wouldn't say that. After all, goalkeepers are supposed to be crazy, aren't they?"

"This one's not crazy," I said, "he's a criminal bloody lunatic." It was no good talking to him, though, or to any of them. As long as a player did his stuff on the field and touched his cap to the directors, he could murder his own grandmother for all they cared.

By this time Jim Mason was fit again, but the way Wilkins had been playing I couldn't have put him out of the team, much though I would have liked to. In fact between you and me I couldn't wait to get him out of the club; it had come around to the point that I was hoping he'd have a bad run. He didn't, though; you had to hand him that, he was a good 'keeper. Afraid of nothing, although there was barely eleven stone of him, and much more judgment and knowledge of angles than you'd ever have given him credit for the way he behaved off the field – and on it too, if it came to that.

Still, if he was playing well, the kids he was taking around with him weren't, and it was easy to tell why; they were coming in for training in the morning with great rings round their eyes. With Wilkins you could never tell; he always looked as if he'd been up all night, even when we were down at Brighton for special training, playing golf and getting the sea breeze.

I decided the best way to deal with it was to talk to the lads he was leading astray. There were three of them, and I had them into the office together and gave them a pep talk, nothing severe, more like a father putting his kids on the right path. I told them I knew what they were up to, I knew who was responsible, and it was affecting their play. If it went on I was going to drop both of them that were in the first team and take them off top money – the other one was in the reserves, and I'd dock his pay as well. They all shuffled about a bit, but in the end they said, "All right, Mr. Jones," and I let them go.

"Now mind you be good boys," I said, "because if there's any more of this carry on, you'll be the ones who're going to suffer, not me."

The next morning in comes Wilkins and asks for a transfer. I nearly shook hands with him. Anyway I tried to make out like I was worried and I asked him what he wanted a transfer for.

"You're against me," he said, "you think I'm a bad influence."

"If you want the truth," I said, "I think you are."

"You were always against me," he said, "you'd judged me before I'd played one bloody game for this club."

"Now look here," I said, "when you arrived here, I told you that as far as I was concerned, you began with a clean sheet, and I meant it. But I'm not going to have you getting my young players into bad habits."

"Why do I always get blamed ?" he said. "Just because we all happened to go along to the same places together."

"I know those places," I said, "and I know these kids only started to go to them after you arrived."

"Well, I want you to put me on the list," he says.

Would you believe it, I bring it up at the next board meeting and the directors say no. Mind you, I'd half expected it.

"You can't let him go," Maxwell says, "look at the way he's playing."

Old Radford backs him up as usual, wheezing away in between polishing off the whisky. "The boy's done well. Best buy we've made for seasons."

"Look here, Mr. Radford," I said, "you only see him when he's playing. I've got to judge a player by what effect he has on the others, as well, and this bloke's a bad influence on the young players."

"Nonsense, nonsense," he says, "perfectly nice lad. I've spoken to him many a time."

"What do you think he's going to do?" I asked him, "start blinding and cursing in front of you like he does when he's with the other lads? He may be crackers in some ways, but he's not as far gone as that."

"No, no, Jack," Maxwell says, "you judge the boy too harshly, you must give him time to settle down." There were one or two things I'd have liked to say to that, but I didn't say any of them: I just simply pointed out that if ever he got properly settled down, you could say goodbye to club discipline, team spirit and the whole damn works. It didn't have any effect on them, though. The boy was playing well, and what happened other than that wasn't their worry: it was my job to carry the can and keep everybody happy. I felt like telling them they wanted a psychologist, not just an ordinary manager, or maybe I should have said a prison governor.

So the next day I have him along and I tell him his transfer hasn't been granted. "It's not my fault," I said, "so you needn't blame me," and he said – like I knew he would – "No, I know you don't want me here, you never bleeding did. I'll come back soon and I'll ask again."

"All right," I said, "but you'll get the same answer, you'll see." For a moment I felt like telling him that if he really wanted to get away, the best method was to play a couple of stinkers, but there are limits. Instead of which, of course, he went on playing well, almost as if he was doing it out of spite. We had a cup tie that week, away to Preston, and it was bound to be a hard one: they'd been playing well at home and scoring a lot of goals.

On form, they should have eaten us, but we got a quick goal, and after that Wilkins practically kept them out on his own – it was the best he'd played for us yet. Old Maxwell came snuffling up to me afterwards, grinning all over his face, and said, "You see how right we were, Jack? We can't transfer him now, can we?" What could you say?

Well, we all got on to the London train, we were in the restaurant car feeling, you know, nice and happy and Radford and his hangers-on were putting away the whisky till honestly I'd've thought it would be running out of their ears. All the directors were coming up to Wilkins one after another and saying, "Well played, Don, we've got you to thank," and him just sitting there with a beer in front of him, looking down at the table as though they were telling him off instead of congratulating him, although I did catch him smiling to himself now and again, just a quick one when he thought nobody was looking.

Maybe I should have been keeping an eye on him, because it turned out afterwards he'd gone through more than a dozen bottles. Anyway, about three quarters-of-an-hour later I suddenly hear him shouting, effing this and effing that, and when I turn round I see him arguing with the dining-car attendant. He said later the man insulted him; the boys told me that he just said politely he couldn't bring him any more beer, because the second service was coming up.

I got up from where I was sitting but unfortunately Maxwell was sitting between me and the gangway, and before I could get across, Wilkins had hit the bloke. Gerry and someone else grabbed him before he could do any more, but the waiter had his hands over his face and blood was coming through from his nose and I knew we were in for trouble. That Wilkins was a vicious little bastard when he was drunk, and now he was shouting and carrying on so that everyone in the diner was standing up and looking. I told him to shut his mouth, he'd caused enough trouble already, and he toned it down to just mumbling and grumbling.

The waiter wasn't badly hurt; Joey Thomas, our trainer, mopped him up with some water and a serviette, but the chief attendant was cutting up nasty, "Something will have to be done about this, I'm afraid. The police will have to be told." But when I got a chance I took the bloke who'd been hit aside and said, "Look, you don't want to ruin the boy's career, do you? He's a nice lad" – I'm glad I couldn't see my own face when I said that – "and he doesn't mean any harm. He'd played a marvellous game, and he just overdid the celebration, that's all. If you bring a charge, what good will it do you? If you drop it, the club will see you're all right."

Anyhow, after a while he agreed to take a tenner and then I had to worry about the press – thank the Lord there was only one of them eating with us and he was pretty new, so I could scare him a bit – he'd just come on the Gazette.

"Listen, son," I told him, "you work with me and I work with you. If you forget about this I'll see you don't lose by it; the first good story I've got, I'll come to you. But put a word about this in the paper and you and I are finished, understand? I don't ever want to see you at the ground." I didn't want to talk like that, he seemed a nice enough kid, but what could I do? He hummed and hawed a bit, very upset, then he said that if his paper didn't get it and someone else did, he'd be in trouble.

"I'll see that no one else gets it," I told him – though I was dead worried – "you can rely on me for that," and in the end I managed to talk him round.

Well if it did one thing, all this, it shook the board back on their heels – all four of them. That Monday they called a special meeting about it. Mind you, I knew what was going to come of it before it ever began – they wouldn't let him go after a blinder like he'd played at Preston, so they'd give him another chance, then they'd all go home and congratulate themselves for being so big hearted. Which was exactly what they did.

As for Wilkins himself, he was more worried than anybody. "It's my wife," he kept saying to me, on the Monday – and I could see he must have sweated it out going through Sunday's papers and waiting for Monday's. "I don't care what they do to me but I just don't want my wife to know."

"Well I won't tell her," I said, "and I don't suppose any of the papers are going to mention it now," but I could see he was still worrying. It surprised me, him running round the West End after tarts all week, and then worrying himself stiff about upsetting his wife. I said if he cared about her as much as that, why didn't he change his ways a bit, and he flared up at me, "That hasn't got nothing to bloody well do with it, that's my personal life!"

It seemed to me it had everything to do with it, but I didn't say anything more. I'd met his wife a few times and she seemed a nice enough kid, too good for him; Welsh and dark haired and quite pretty in a plumpish sort of way. I knew he was a bit of a trial to her as well because she said to me one day, "Oh, Mr. Jones, you've no idea what I have to put up with at times."

"Well," I said, "we'd better compare notes, because there's times when I think he's going to turn my blinking hair grey."

That waiter business seemed to scare him a bit and we had a little peace for the next couple of weeks. He was still playing well, and we got through the next round of the Cup all right, at home to Liverpool, and I thought things were maybe changing for the better. As far as I could make out, the others weren't going round Soho with him any more, which was something. Most of the older players still didn't like him any better – they didn't like the language he used in front of their wives, for one thing; you couldn't blame them – and I think there was a bit of resentment because he was keeping Jim Mason out of the side: the old Trade Union spirit.

Still, they couldn't complain about the way he was playing – better and better every week – and when Wales played Ireland in Belfast, nobody was surprised when he was picked. It was his first cap for over two years; the Welsh selectors were meant to have said they'd never choose him again after things he was supposed to have done on tour – getting drunk, and something about a maid in a hotel – but they couldn't leave him out on this form.

By this time we were in the semi-final, playing Burnley at Villa Park, and we beat them 3-1. The whole team was playing really well and the defence was showing tremendous confidence, like they knew that playing in front of Wilkins they couldn't very well go wrong. There'd been no more talk of a transfer from him. That Welsh cap had sweetened him, I could tell, and I knew he'd been keeping his eye on the Cup Final, too; not just the honour and that sort of talk, but all the perks, that went with being a finalist. There were no flies on him.

So he was behaving himself for a change and he was just praying it would hold out at least until after Wembley. Wolves were the other team and they'd been made favourites; we didn't mind that because we knew as far as finals were concerned, it meant sweet Fanny Adams. We went down to Brighton again for special training, and the Friday before the match I brought the team up to town – we stayed at a hotel on the North Circular Road. We took a quiet day, just a short work out with the ball, a tactical discussion, then billiards and snooker and a spot of cards. I'd told the lads I wanted them all in bed by ten o'clock, but at ten fifteen Wilkins and the two kids he'd been taking round with him still hadn't turned up, and I was beginning to get worried.

At quarter-to-twelve they still weren't there. I'd phoned their homes, I'd phoned the hospitals and now I was trying to phone round to clubs and places they were likely to be. Radford was still with me; he'd come along to have dinner with the team, and when this happened he'd stayed to see how it would turn out: he'd rung up the chairman, too.

Soon after quarter-to-twelve they do roll in, the two boys holding Wilkins up, one on either arm. He was dead drunk, could hardly walk, or talk for that matter, and what you could hear him saying was just cursing and blinding. The boys looked very sheepish, and I could see what had happened – it could wait till after the final, there was no point in upsetting everything now.

"All right," I said, "get him to bed, you two; we'll talk about this in the morning." I thought Radford would have the sense to leave it alone for now, but he wouldn't – anyway, he'd had one or two himself. He came up to Wilkins, absolutely shaking he was, though don't ask me whether it was with rage or with drink, and he said, "You ought to be ashamed of yourself, the night before the final. You're a disgrace to the club."

Wilkins looked up at him, his eyes sort of slowly rolled round, and he said, "You effing old so-and-so, as if you don't take a bottle of whisky to bed with you every night – and I bet the club has to pay for it, too."

Radford just stood there, he was speechless, and I'd got nothing to say either. I couldn't help thinking there was a lot of truth in what Wilkins had said, I'd been wanting to say something like it myself for years, but he was finished as far as our club was concerned.

I told him so the next morning when he came to see me, very fed up and repentant. "You can do anything in this club and maybe get away with it," I said, "except insult a director. Directors are sacred."

"I didn't mean nothing," he said, "I was blind drunk, I didn't even know what happened till Charlie told me. Please, Mr. Jones, give me another chance. I want to stay with this club, I'm happy here; I'll go and apologise to Mr. Radford."

"You can try if you like," I said, "but it isn't likely to get you very far. I'd steer clear of him for the moment, if I was you." He was just going out of the room very slowly when I thought of something and said, "There's only one thing that can save you, my boy."

"What's that?" he asks.

"Play a blinder in the final this afternoon."

The directors came and had lunch in the hotel, and they talked about nothing else all through the meal. Radford wanted to drop him – now, at the last moment – but the others put their foot down at that, and I'd have walked out myself if they'd ever done anything so crazy. I had my eye on Wilkins. He didn't say much and he hardly ate, and I was afraid of what was going to happen at Wembley.

Anyway, we started well enough. After we'd got through all the bands and the handshakes and the waiting and all that bloody nerve racking twaddle that can lose you a match at Wembley before you've even begun, we settled down nicely and we were a goal up in ten minutes. They rubbed that one off just before half-time – a good one; Wilkins was drawn out of his goal by their left winger, and he didn't have a chance.

At half-time in the dressing-room he looked a bit more cheerful: I told him he wasn't to blame, and said they were to keep on like they were, we had them going.

We'd played forty minutes of the second half without another goal being scored, and it looked a certainty there'd be extra time. That didn't worry me because I knew we were a younger side than they were and the longer it went, the better it was for us. Old Maxwell was babbling away, "We were right to keep Wilkins in, Radford, he's played well, you can't deny he's played well," and old Radford could only mumble at him – he couldn't very well disagree.

Then their right winger crossed a high ball; nothing very dangerous, Wilkins had been eating those up right through the game and besides, their centre-forward was out of position. He came out to his six yard line, he jumped for the ball – and then he must have taken his eye off it, because the next thing you knew it had slipped out of his hands and rolled across the goal and their inside-left had walked it in.

I sat there with my head in my hands and honest to God I felt sick: it was cruel. I could hear Radford saying, "I told you, I told you," then I looked up again and Wilkins was rolling about on the ground holding his face like he was in agony.

He'd never kick another ball for the club, I knew that. The funny thing about it is that in some odd way, I was sorry.

The agents

When I lifted the telephone a voice cried, as though springing an ecstatic surprise, "*Ciao, Brian! Sono Beppe!*"

"*Ciao, come stai?*" I said, and wondered what he wanted.

"It's so long since we've seen each other!" he pursued, in Italian, still fortissimo, with his strong, southern accent. "I arrived in London yesterday. When shall we meet? What are you doing now? Come here to my hotel, and we'll have lunch!"

"Which hotel?"

"The usual one," he said, reproachfully; I realised that I should have known. "The Oxford Towers."

When I came into the foyer, his plump little figure came bouncing across the carpets to meet me, the huge eyes full of a conscious, qualified sincerity. "*Ciao, caro!*" he said, enfolding my hand in his cushioned hand. There was enough restraint in the performance to remind me of what had been implied on the telephone, the projection of a personality.

"Brian!" Now he spoke in English, taking my arm. "We don't meet enough. You know, when I see you, I see Italy, I think I'm in Rome again; you know? Really!"

I might have reciprocated, for in Beppe, too, I saw Italy; or rather, a perpetual aspect of Italy: the deprived South, transcending itself, with its driving need to cut *la bella figura*. I noticed that he'd put on weight; there was more flesh at the jowls, signs of indulgence. His suit was the best I had seen him in, and he smelled a little of toilet water. "When I'm with *you*, Brian, I think I'm in Piazza di Spagna! Honestly!"

When I'm with you, Beppe, I think I'm in Foggia. But I did not say this to him. I had known him for years, known him when he was up and when he was down; when he was scratching a living as an interpreter, when he was driving a scarlet Alfa Romeo through Rome like a scourge, when he was the whipping-boy of Naples – the team was doing badly, and he had engaged their new players. Since then, he had brought off his coup, the signing of McDougald, the Scottish winger, for Internazionale. McDougald was now the hero of Milan and Beppe, flourishing in his wake, had set upon himself a new and higher valuation, at which the world was expected to take him, too.

We drank Chianti with our lunch. When we had finished, Beppe smoked a cigar, and it was only then, as he sensuously exhaled, that he asked, "Do you know Bill Vining?"

"Pretty well," I said.

"You think he's a good boy? I mean, the sort of player who'd do well in Italy?"

"His club would never let him go." Beppe shrugged with one plump shoulder. "*Vedremo, eh*? We'll see."

"He'd certainly do well, if you could get him."

"How much do you think they'd want? His club, I mean."

"About a hundred thousand – if they were prepared to part at all."

This did not seem to discourage him. He was clearly working for a very rich club indeed.

"Brian, tell him he should come to Trastevere. You know Rome. I mean, you tell him what a wonderful thing he'd do. He'd get everything. I'm not joking. Car, apartment, marvellous bonuses."

"Beppe, I'm a journalist," I said, feeling the humbug and temporiser that I knew he'd take me for. "Very well," he said – now in Italian again – "you're a journalist, but you can mention it to him. There's no harm in that, is there?"

"I'd rather not."

"For me. As a favour. You're a friend of mine. Try to convince him."

"How can I? The manager's a friend of mine as well." Besides, who would throw any green young Englishman into the cauldron of Roman football, with its serpentine intrigues, its hysteric Press, the gilded temptations of Via Veneto?

"Brian, you disappoint me."

"I'm very sorry."

"I thought you were my friend."

"I am."

"Rovers won't lose. We'll pay them anything they want – even a hundred thousand pounds. Vining may never have another chance like this in all his life."

"He'd certainly make a lot of money."

"Tell him, then!" Beppe leaned across the table; he put his hand on mine, his eyes were full of sincerity and a liquid appeal.

"Yes, I'll gladly tell him *that*, Beppe, when I see him."

"*Sei il mio amico.*"

As we took our leave, outside the hotel, he looked up at me and begged, "But you won't write anything about this?"

"Of course not."

"Good, good, your word... I always trust you. And you'll have the story first, I promise you. Before everyone. *Ciao, caro.*"

Maurizio arrived at the end of that week. He, too, saluted me by telephone. "You're here for Vining," I said.

"Oh! Who told you?"

"You must be. Beppe Valentini's here as well."

"*Ma no!* How long has he been here?"

"Only a few days. He's working for Trastevere."

"I know, I know. *Ha combinato qualcosa?* Has he fixed anything?"

"I don't think so."

"Let's hope not, let's hope not. Can I meet you? As soon as possible? It's very important."

"Of course..."

"Of course not."

We met that afternoon, outside a public house in Soho. I arrived there first, and was able thus to see Maurizio as he came round a corner, wrapped in his air of constant conspiracy, his eyes darting like astonished fish. He was tall and very thin and his face was that of a melancholy fox, its sadness somehow emphasised by his long, bony nose; his hair was cropped in a style that did not suit him. He greeted me with nervous delight, his lean hand pumping mine, "*Mi fa piacere.*" At closer quarters, he seemed too vulnerable, too confused and innocent, for successful intrigue, as if doomed to remain the pawn, the put-upon. And yet he got things done, I knew it; blundering in where angels feared to tread, God's fool, outflanking those who laughed at him.

"This way!" he said, and guided me down a side street. "I don't want to go past that café – the one with the waiters. If they see me, they'll know; the news will be all over Milan by this evening."

I glanced over my shoulder. As usual, the café's clients had overflowed on to the pavement, where they were shouting amiably at one another in the way of the piazza. Passing by, one always heard the words, "Juventus... Milan... Inter."

We walked down into Shaftesbury Avenue, and along Piccadilly to Green Park. "You're here for Milan, then?" I asked him.

"No, no, I swear to you."

"Then who?" Maurizio ducked his head, gave his strange giggle, looked at me out of the corner of his eye, and said, "For Ambrosiana."

There was, I thought, a symmetry about it all, for if Trastevere were the third force among the Roman clubs, then Ambrosiana were the third force in Milan.

It was Spring, but the foliage of the plane trees had yet to burst forth and transform the park; for the moment it lay bare and unprotected, under a premature sun. Here and there, tramps were asleep on the resilient grass, and courting couples were whispering, to transistor radios. We found two deck-chairs and Maurizio sat restlessly, his long fingers plucking now and then at the lapel of his well-cut overcoat. "Do you think I'll succeed?" he asked. I thought it most unlikely, even impossible, but he'd surprised me before. "Perhaps."

"I want your advice," he said.

"On how to get hold of Vining?"

"No, no, I know that. I saw him this morning," and he gave me a furtive smile, as if half proud and half ashamed.

"You're a phenomenon, Maurizio. What did he say?"

"*Insomma*... He said he's very interested, but he didn't mention Valentini. Do you think he's a serious boy?"

"Yes, as far as I know. You haven't talked to the club at all?"

"*Perbacco!*" he said, and giggled. The agent's approach was invariable; rational, Latin and illicit. If the club were approached, the club said no; the method, therefore, was to go to the player, planting the seeds of ambition. "But has Valentini spoken to Vining? Do you know?"

"I should think he must have done by now."

"Then it's getting serious," Maurizio said. "But I think if Vining's sensible he'll come to Milan and not to Rome." He darted me a glance. "Don't you think so?"

"It's easier to play there, certainly."

"And the money. Celio doesn't mind what he offers. You know he makes armaments? You know he's almost as big as Berretta?"

"Yes."

"But how can I convince Vining? If you could tell him." I was silent; Maurizio was silent, too. At length he said, looking towards St James'. "It isn't that I want to worry you... He knows you've lived in Italy. He said, yes, I like him, I know him well. You know that I don't like to ask you..."

"It's a bit difficult, Maurizio."

"Yes, yes, and then there's another difficulty; he's got an agent."

"An agent? Who?"

"*Ma*... A peasant. A good-for-nothing... A great big man with a red face."

"Jack Collins?"

"You know him?"

"Yes," I said, and I began to laugh. Whatever my surprise, the description had been inescapable. Until a year ago, Collins had been the Rovers' coach, a term which covered his actual function as the club's "finger man", offering illegal inducements to amateurs and schoolboy stars, pounds of steak and overcoats to their parents. It was he who had "discovered" Vining, or rather, had hooked him for the club, after he had been seen on a million television screens, in a schoolboy international match at Wembley. Now, Collins was running a sweet shop in the Mile End Road. It was he who was the third agent to telephone me.

"You'll never guess who this is!" he said, in his high, plaintive, fat man's voice. I guessed. "Well, you'll never guess what it's about." I guessed again. "That's right," he said, with shocked alarm, "but you'll keep it dark? You won't be writing about it, will you?"

"No."

"Brian, Bill and I would like to meet you. We'd like to have a talk to you; we think you can help us. I mean, knowing these places. You've lived there. We haven't lived there, Brian."

We met the following evening, above his sweet shop; his lean wife greeted me, and disappeared. There were encyclopaedias in a bookcase, a dim cabinet of unused china." He's got to have somebody to look after him, Brian," Collins said, as though I had impugned him. "He's only a young boy, he wouldn't know *where* he is, so naturally he came to me." He sat down, hitching his trousers above his high, black, massive boots; his great pink face was full of a resentful innocence. "He knows I looked after him when he came to Rovers."

"Of course," I said.

"The boy knows that. He admits it. He was very upset when I left. I mean, you'd never believe it, Brian, if I told you some of the diabolical things that have gone on." The door bell rang below. "That'll be Bill," said Collins, and heaved from his chair to lumber downstairs.

When he returned, Vining was with him. "Hallo, Brian," he said, greeting me with a certain wary goodwill, which he'd acquired since he had become famous. He was not particularly tall or broad – least of all for a centre-forward – but there was a spare, balanced quality about his whole body, as though every inch and ounce were turned to use. His cheeks were still the rosy cheeks of a boy, his blond hair was combed and creamed into a graduation of elaborate waves, and he had about him the Cockney's alert self-possession. "All right, then?" he said.

"I'm all right," I said. "I've kept hearing about you, all this week."

"Yeah," he said, "Jackie told me." Collins offered us a drink, but Vining refused. "The thing is, Brian," Collins said, "which are we to choose?"

"Do you really want to go, Bill?" I asked.

"You got to think about the money," he said, with a grave, almost mystic, conviction.

"Why should he stay here?" asked Collins, all high-pitched sincerity – as though he were on a platform. "What does he get for it? Twenty quid a week, and at the end of it they throw him on the scrapheap, just like they done to me!"

Vining said nothing. He sat there, legs apart, wearing his cocky, characteristic, good-humoured grin.

"My view is," said Collins, "we ought to choose the one that gives the most money. The one that makes the biggest bid gets him, that's sensible, but I just want to be sure there aren't no snags, that I wouldn't know about and you *might*."

"They might both go and offer the same money," Vining said.

"They might both get turned down," I answered.

"Oh, no, they won't," said Collins, "*we'll* see to it. If the Rovers won't let him go, he'll refuse to sign on for next season, won't you, Billy? Then they'll have to give in, if they see he's really got his mind made up."

"They don't have to. If they're obstinate, they can keep him hanging on for weeks without any wages."

"They'll have to transfer him," Collins said, "they got no alternative. They'd have the Press and the whole country against them. They'd *have* to climb down."

"Well, if they do climb down, your best bet is Milan."

"I fancy Rome, meself," said Vining. I told him why I thought he was wrong. "I don't know," he said, "I mean, all them Roman women. Smashing. We was there last year, on a tour."

"Yes, but Brian *knows*, Bill," Collins said. "You want to listen to him."

For a week, I heard no more. Then, on the front page of my morning newspaper, a headline confronted me: ITALIAN CLUB BIDS £100,000 FOR BILL VINING. Beneath it, there was chapter and verse; that the club was Ambrosiana, of Milan, that their agent, Signor Maurizio Giovannini, was empowered to offer £100,000 for Vining, that the player himself would receive £20,000 for a three-year contract. An hour later, Maurizio himself was on the 'phone, hurried and alarmed.

"*Ciao, sono Maurizio. Come stai?*"

"All right," I answered coldly, in English, "and you?"

"Nobbad." His English was impervious to time and use. "You've seen the newspaper?"

"Yes."

"But listen, it wasn't my fault. I swear to you – on the head of my son."

"I believe you, I believe you."

"You know what happened? Dan Maycock telephoned me" – it was Maycock who had written the story.

"How did he know you were in London?"

"I've no idea."

"Perhaps he'd spoken to Bill, and Bill told him?"

"No, no, he phoned Bill and Bill wouldn't tell him anything. I've talked to him."

"Collins, then."

"*Possibile, possibile...* but I don't think so."

"Then what did you say to him? "

"Nothing, *ti giuro*. He said he'd heard I was over here looking for a player, for one of the Milan clubs, and I said no, no, I'm just thinking of opening another cinema, like the one I had in Wimbledon. Then he said, I heard you were after a London player for Milan, and I said no, no, I'm not working for Milan any more, so he said, then it must be Inter, and I said no, it isn't Inter, so then he laughed and said, it must be Ambrosiana, then, and I said, why should it be? Then he said, well, can you tell me if there's any particular player you're looking at, and I said, well, there might be, just *looking* at them, and he said, is it an inside-forward, and I said no, it's not an inside-forward; so he said, is it a winger, and I said no, it isn't, and he said, well, then, it must be a centre-forward; it must be David Herd, of Arsenal, and I said, no, no, he isn't Scottish. Then he must be English, he said; you know how he laughs when he wants to find something out; very false – it must be Billy Vining, and I said, you're joking. Then he said, suppose it was Billy, how much would an Italian club pay for him? And I said, one of the rich ones? I don't know; about £100,000."

"I see," I said.

"You think I've been indiscreet?"

"Perhaps a little."

"I'm worried about what they'll think in Milan. They'll think I'm a blabber-mouth."

"Why should they?"

"And Rovers will be angry; they'll think I've approached the player."

"Don't worry about it; it had to come out sooner or later."

I telephoned Beppe at once. "*Ma quel cretino!*" he cried. "That idiot-face! Did you know he was here?"

"I'd heard he was."

"But why didn't you tell me? You're my friend! Does he know *I'm* here? "

"I think so."

"This ruins everything! It'll become an auction! And anyway, Ambrosiana can't afford £100,000 They're in debt! This President has guaranteed their overdraft, otherwise they'd have gone into liquidation; the Federation would have put a commissar in. *Che cazzo vogliono fare?* Tell Bill! Tell him when you see him he'd be mad to go to Ambrosiana; they haven't the money to pay him! In any case, who wants to go to Milan when they can come to Rome?"

"I believe he thinks so, too."

"*Ecco!* Then you've spoken to him? "

"Yes."

"What did he say?"

"That he liked the idea of Rome."

"And you told him he should come to Rome?"

"I can't remember."

"*Porca miseria!* Listen; you won't write anything about me, will you?"

"No."

"You're the first I'll give the story to, I promise."

The evening papers carried the news that Valentini was in London. They also reported that Joe Withingon, the Rovers' manager, had said that his club was determined to keep Vining. Vining had said he knew nothing about it; if it was true, then of course he would have to think about it seriously.

I took him out to lunch the following day at a French restaurant in Soho. Its one large room had an air of dim and muted expense; Vining looked about it with bright, interested eyes. He was wearing a tie-less blue jersey-shirt, with pointed collars.

"Do you like it?" I asked.

"Yeah, Brian, I do, it's all right."

"What'll you eat?"

"You choose, Brian, I don't know." I gave our order to the sad, middle-aged waiter, whose dress-clothes hung wearily upon him, a melancholy gesture.

"You think I'd do all right out there, Brian?" Vining asked.

"Of course you would," I said, with surprise. On a football field he was confidence personified, barely twenty years old, yet capable for the past two years of bursting, swerving and side-stepping past a defence as though it wasn't there.

"What makes you think so, Brian?"

"Well," I said, "I think you're unique; like Jimmy Greaves, or Pele of Brazil. You can score goals that look impossible until you've scored them."

"Yeah, thanks," he said, and looked gravely unconvinced. "Still, I got to go, haven't I? One or the other of them. You got to think of your future; I might never have another chance like this one again. I mean, you break a leg you're out, aren't you? You're forgotten."

"I know."

"Jack's got it worked out; he reckons Rovers will have to let me go."

"They don't *have* to," I said. "I'm afraid that's where the snag is."

"If they see I'm determined, if I say I'm never going to kick another ball for them."

"They can still hang on. You could lose a lot of money."

"Yeah, well I gone into that, you see. I mean, don't tell nobody, but if I go to this Trastevere, Beppe's said they'll make up anything I lose, and Jackie knows a bloke that'll give me a job to see me over."

"Well, it's a risk," I said.

"Yeah, but it's a risk I got to take, though, ain't it, Brian?"

"You can give up enjoying football; you know that? You'll get kicked there."

"I got away with it here so far though, haven't I? Anyway, it's worth it. You know when you go somewhere else there's going to be things you got to put up with, don't you? "

"I still think Milan's the better bet."

He shrugged. "I'll just have to wait and see what turns up. Anyhow, I'm leaving that side of it to Jack at the moment."

"What does Joe Withington say?"

"What, old Joe? He had me in there and he said, you seen these agents, haven't you? And I said, well, they seen Jack; and he said, you can tell Jack to keep his nose out of this, I don't care if he is your agent, it's none of his bloody business. He said, as far as I'm concerned, we haven't had no official approach, and if we do get one, I'm turning it down."

"And what did you say to that?"

"I didn't say nothing, I don't want to fall out with him now, do I? If I leave him alone, he might come round, he might change his mind."

"Why do you need an agent at all?"

"I got to have somebody to look after me, haven't I?"

The following Saturday, he scored three brilliant goals at Wolverhampton, and I travelled back with Rovers' party, on the train.

"How can I let him go, Brian?" Withington said. The meal was over, and I had sat down opposite him, in the empty seat at his table. A few tables away, Vining and a half a dozen others were noisily playing brag. "How can I be expected to?" Withington could be melancholy or effervescent, and now he was in one of his tired, depressive moods; his heavy eyelids looked like small, brown, wrinkled egg-shells. "And this Collins, he's a villain. All he wants is to do the club down, because I gave him the sack when I went there."

"It's turning down a lot of money, isn't it? You're not a rich club."

"I know we're not, but if we sell him, how are we going to replace him? Anyone we go to for a player will know we're coming, for a start. They'll be waiting for us."

"Have you seen the agents?"

"I've seen them both; little Valentini and the other one, the fox-faced one, as well. I said, if you want to make a bid, you send someone over from the club. I don't deal with agents."

It was thus that Gaudenzio arrived.

I called on him at the Oxford Towers, on the morning he flew into London. Valentini had momentarily gone out and, sitting there, Gaudenzio looked swarthily exotic, torn out of that Roman context where I'd always met him, where he was merely part of a surrealist landscape. His round, dark, fleshy face, grey hair brushed neatly back above it, wore, not its usual, satyr's joviality, but a look of vulnerable surprise, barely qualified even by his eternal monocle. At the same time, the monocle, the tieless, dark green jersey, the swaggering cut of his suit, the pointed shoes, gave him his usual touch of the buccaneer. He had been a director of Trastevere when I lived in Rome; now,

40

he was Vice-President, a man of infinite viability and impenetrable background.

He greeted me with joyful relief. "Here in London," he complained, in his loud, rough voice, "there's nobody that speaks Italian, no one." He ordered me a drink, toasted me, and asked, "This Vining, do you think we'll get him?"

"You might," I said. "It will be difficult."

"But isn't there someone at the club we can give something to?"

"Not the manager. He's incorruptible."

"In that case, it becomes serious. But you think he's really a great player? You've seen him? He'd do well in Italy? We can give him everything; you know that – a flat, bonuses, everything. And Valentini? You think he's the right man? Do they think he's the right man? Do they think well of him here? Yes? Then if they think well of him, why do they insist that I come? What about this other man, this Giovannini? Is he good? Perhaps we'd do better with *him*?" He had brought Rome with him, into the hotel lounge. Suddenly the moral climate had changed, and all was Latin light and realism.

"And this Vining has an agent, too. Perhaps we should give something to him."

"If you like."

"According to you, what ought we to do?"

"Go and see Joe Withington, the manager, and make your offer."

"You think so, you think so?" he said, and then, the sun emerging from behind a cloud of meditation, "*Il nostro carissimo Brian!* Always a friend of Trastevere!"

The story broke the following Monday morning; Vining was going to Trastevere. Reading it, I had a feeling of betrayal and bewilderment. Gaudenzio had indeed brought Rome to London with him; logic and inevitability had gone to the winds. It was as though one had carefully assembled the ingredients of a Dundee cake, only to draw out of the oven a steak and kidney pie. Someone had lied to me; someone had wavered. I grimly prepared for the inevitable telephone calls.

Collins was the first, but his voice, instead of being exuberant, was more bitterly aggrieved than ever. "You'll never believe this! The most diabolical thing!... It wasn't my fault; if it had been up to me, I'd have given you the story before everyone. They did it all without me; I didn't even get consulted! Yes! And I'm his agent! Mind you, I don't think it's Billy, I don't think it's *him* at all, I been on to him; it's *them*, it's Rovers, that Joe Withington. Well they'll pay for it, I can tell you! Honestly, Brian, I know so much about that club, I could get them thrown out of the Football League! I'm going to tell Withington; if they still try it on, I'll publish everything. You don't think your paper would be interested, Brian?"

"I don't think so, Jack."

Next, there was Maurizio, incredulous and dismayed. "Do you believe it?"

"Yes."

"*Ma no*, it isn't possible. I spoke to Collins yesterday, and he promised me..."

I met Beppe at Tottenham that Wednesday, before the start of a floodlit match; in the great car-park, where the Bentleys and Jaguars nosed their way between the little groups of talking players, and where the fat, swarthy men stood with cigars pointing arrogantly from their mouths, like guns from the turrets of a battleship.

"*Hai visto? hai visto?*" he cried, "you've seen what I've done?"

"Yes," I said. "*Complimenti*."

"Brian, I wanted to give you the story, but I couldn't find you. I rang you; I rang your home."

"I couldn't have been in."

"We'll go out and celebrate, eh? You and I and Billy. We'll go to the Pigalle; they've got a wonderful show there, you know?" He was up; higher up than I had ever known him; it was a moment when he and his projected image met, so that it became almost real. "Because when you go out with Beppe, you know you have a good time! You laugh, you sing!"

"I know." I wanted, now, a respite from all of them; from Beppe's loud euphoria, Maurizio's agitation, Collins' high-pitched complaint, Vining's devious immaturity. Withington, when I saw him again, told me in his tired way, "I couldn't really do much about it, Brian, once I saw the boy was determined to hold out. I mean, he'd got a job lined up, we'd probably be without him for two or three months at least, next season, he'd have that on his mind till the end of this one, and to tell the truth, I don't know whether we're entitled to stop him making all that money. You're only going to have a discontented player, and I'd rather have an ordinary player that's trying than a star that won't give you anything. We've said we'll let him go at the end of the season; we're not going to sign anything till then."

In May, a week after the Cup Final, I went to Rome on holiday. The city was enjoying the full glory of its Spring; the strong sunlight played on warm, russet stone, on the leaves of the plane trees by the Tiber, on the great, terraced sweep of the Spanish Steps; football seemed an obscenity and an irrelevance.

When I had been there three days, however, conscience and duty moved me; I telephoned Gaudenzio, who jubilantly invited me to dinner that evening in Piazza Navona.

The long, elegant *piazza* was in twilight when I got there; outside the appointed restaurant, a long table had been set, but Gaudenzio was nowhere to be seen. I waited unresentfully; it was still and quiet, and from time to time, interspersed between the knives and forks and voices, one could hear the calm, steady play of the fountains.

In half an hour, a car drew up, a black Lancia, and Gaudenzio sprang from it exuberantly into the square, his shouting and his laughter assaulting the quietness. As he made towards the restaurant, his movements were not so much a walk as the jaunty, shoulder-swinging parody of a walk. After him came three tall, young, elegant men in slacks and blazers, and scarcely had he greeted me, arms outspread to postulate delight, than another car had pulled up, with a scream and a skid, and more young men were following. Together, bearing me with them, they erupted on to the terrace of the restaurant. Over them all, Gaudenzio presided like a wicked Bacchus.

"Our very dear Brian!" he presented me to them, "journalist from London; a city full of beautiful women." And he blew a kiss into the night. "*Ma no, ma no!* It's true, I was astonished, dizzied."

"And this Vining?" an elegant, crew-cut young man asked me; I saw that he was wearing in his button-hole the green and white enamelled badge of Trastevere. "Can he really play?"

"Tell them, Brian," Gaudenzio cried, his round head turning, his monocle flashing and winking as it caught the light, "tell them his shots are like the thunder of God! That he bursts away like a Sputnik!" There was a chorus of laughter and ridicule. "True or not, Brian?" Gaudenzio cried.

"More or less," I said.

"There; did you hear that?" He ordered Frascati, and ham and figs for everybody. "What figs, boys, eh? *Che fichi, eh raegazzi?*" and this provided him with his refrain, all through the dinner, "*Che fichi, eh, che fichi?*" the gruff voice full of relish and suggestion. He initiated an elaborate drinking game – "I drink to the health of Sub-Lieutenant Beppe. *Evviva!*" – full of expanding, repetitive formulae, taps on the table, and ritual wiping of an imaginary moustache. The young man who had asked me about Vining giggled hopelessly, and could not get it right.

"The toast of the evening!" Gaudenzio called out at last, and rose to ironic cries of, "*Bravo ingegnere!* " glass held aloft, "To Bee-ly Vining, who arrives tomorrow; to the goals he's going to score for Trastevere!"

"Coming tomorrow?" I asked him, as he drove me to my hotel.

"*Certo*. With Valentini. He's going to look at the apartment; a most beautiful apartment, in Via Archimede. Then he'll sign the *compromesso*, and afterwards, the Vice-President and I will fly to London, to complete the contract. Come with me to the airport, tomorrow, and you can write about it for your newspaper." I could, indeed. "Phone me in the morning, at Trastevere."

I spent most of the morning trying to unearth him; he had disappeared, as only a Roman can. At Trastevere they said, "The engineer's not here"; nor was he to be found at his apartment. At last, on my fifth call to Trastevere, a new voice told me, "Try Tennis Laziale; the engineer usually goes there for lunch."

The club lay in a road off the Via Flaminia, and was difficult to find. The day was at once hot and overcast, one of those heavy, Roman days on which the sun, emerging at last with afternoon, brings no relief, but only further castigation. Arrived at the club, sweating, my tie and jacket over my arm, I felt as though I were a beggar at a banquet. Around me, all was calm serenity, deck-chairs, elegance, iced drinks. I glimpsed the young man with the Trastevere badge, languid and immaculate in tennis shorts. From his deck-chair, he called to a poised, slim, graceful Roman girl, with long, auburn hair, "Amanda, you're beautiful! If I wasn't married, I'd marry you myself." And she replied, drifting serenely by, "*Certo, e un peso*; it's a burden, certainly." On the terrace of the club house, a dozen men – some of whom had been at dinner in Piazza Navona – were playing cards.

"*Che desidera?*" a steward, white-jacketed, enquired, beside me. "The *ingegnere*? There he is!" and he pointed to a deck-chair where, indeed, I could now see the *ingegnere's* grey, groomed head, reclining half-way down the canvas.

"Gaudenzio!" I said, too low, and got no answer; but the steward moved to tap him on the shoulder, "*Ingegnere!*" Seeing me, he yawned and rose, coming towards me with his jogging walk.

"The 'plane doesn't arrive till four. There's a car coming."

I crept into a deck-chair beside his, and tried to disappear.

"*Bellino, eh?*" he said. "We spend the day here."

The car, driven with relentless, expert speed by a huge, bronzed man in a blue shirt, bowled along the white road to Ciampino, between the endless double rank of hoardings; the cat's eyes, the Cinzano bottles. We were out on the tarmac when the great, glinting silver plane taxied and turned with the slow precision of a clever elephant. Two or three photographers adjusted cameras, a fat Roman journalist in sunglasses took me by the arm and said, "You'll interpret for us, won't you, Glanville?"

The high steps were wheeled up to the aeroplane; at the top, a silver door opened, and a pretty, dark stewardess appeared.

"*Eccolo! Eccolo!*" shouted Gaudenzio, arm, hand, finger pointing with an electric urgency; and now, in the doorway, in white shirtsleeves, stood Bill Vining. Beside him, beaming, tubby and proprietorial, appeared Valentini. As Vining made a movement to go forward, he caught him quickly by the arm, and the cameras clicked, the tableau was saved. In that instant, watching them, the scene, for me, suddenly grew sinister; Valentini's smile, his pose; one hand on Vining's arm; were too much those of the hunter, returning with his prey. Then the scene had gone, Vining was coming down the steps, and Gaudenzio was eagerly moving forward.

"Hallo, Brian!" Vining said, cheerfully unsurprised, as though he, too, regarded his arrival as an event, at which one were expected to be present.

"*Ecco il Presidente!*" Gaudenzio cried as we passed, in cortege, into the reception hall, and the club president it was indeed, a heavy man, tonsured and imperial, with a great stomach, wearing a pleased smile, as though his own significance were a perpetual source of quiet satisfaction. He received Vining with a mumble of cordial, off-handed welcome, as President to subject.

When I got back from my hotel, a voice called me, cautiously, from the penumbra beyond the hallway. I turned, to see it was Maurizio. "*Ciao!* You told me in London that you always stayed here!" His voice remained very low, though the reception desk was deserted, and there was no one to hear us but the fat old *signora* cat-napping in a corner of the sofa.

"What are you doing here, Maurizio?"

He rose from his chair, looking about him, more conspiratorial than ever. "For Vining!" He put a bony finger to his lips. "Can we go to your room?"

We climbed in the narrow, creaking lift. "*Allora...* I'm not disturbing you?"

"Of course not."

"You met Vining at the airport?"

"Yes."

"But I don't think he's signed yet?"

"No."

"*Meno male*, thank goodness."

"He's staying at the Quirinale, if you want to get hold of him."

"I know."

"Maurizio, you know everything."

He giggled. "I've something to tell you. Remaining between me and you."

"Certainly."

"I don't think Vining is going to join Trastevere."

"Then he's going to Ambrosiana?"

"*Speriamo.* Let's hope so."

"*Complimenti.*"

He giggled again and said, "Thank you... But you don't mind telling me of any developments while he's in Rome?"

"Not at all."

"With Trastevere, one has to be on one's toes: especially with Valentini in the middle of things."

"You don't like Valentini."

"*Ma...* not very much." Again, he gave his deprecating giggle. "*Troppo meridionale*, too much of a Southerner."

Ten minutes later, I saw him to the lift, carefully closing its rattling glass gates, "*Ciao, ciao*," he said. The lift shot up, instead of down, suddenly stopped dead, then came down again, to rest once more at my floor. The doors rattled open, framing Maurizio's melancholy face. "I pressed the wrong button," he said.

Early that evening, I made my way up the urban waste of Via Nazionale, stagnant with exhaust fumes. In the hall of the Quirinale a little Italian journalist met me, gesturing towards the lounge. "They're all in session," he said, "the Grand Junta of Trastevere."

They were indeed; huge, sleek, jowly men, in smooth, dark suits, with massive, sloping shoulders – the club insignia in every buttonhole. There was an air of bland menace about them, and, for the second time that day, I felt concerned for Vining; relieved that he might yet be extricated by Maurizio. The directors greeted me courteously, with the sleepy, sated smiles of predatory animals at rest. The President was not among them, but Gaudenzio, who was, told me, "Vining's upstairs. We showed him his apartment; he was very, very impressed by it."

I telephoned Vining from the foyer, and took the lift up to his room where I found him, pink and smiling, sitting on the bed.

"I hear they showed you your apartment," I said.

"Yeah; fabulous, it was."

"You really think you'd like it here?"

"Terrific, Brian."

I wondered if Maurizio's assurances were wish-fulfilment.

"You don't think I'm doing the right thing, do you, Brian?"

"I don't know," I said, "I don't know what you've been offered."

"More than I can refuse – I can't say no more than that."

"I see," I said, and wondered if Maurizio's offer had been made, and overtopped.

Our privacy was ended by a thump on the door, and the boisterous entry of Valentini. "*Ciao, Billy, ciao, Brian.*" He greeted each of us with sententious emphasis. "You want to come with us, Brian; I'm taking Billy in my car, to the club office? It's a nice car, eh, Billy?"

"Fabulous," Vining said.

It was another Alfa-Romeo, blue, this time, chipped and dented with the scars of a hundred minor collisions. Valentini drove on his horn and on his mouth, a *meridionale*, telling Rome he had arrived, cutting in atrociously, taking ludicrous risks, each new escapade concluding with his head stuck out of the window, bellowing abuse.

"He's a boy, isn't he?" Vining chuckled, and from the front seat, Beppe said, "You see, Bill, all of them are madmen here; mad drivers."

"Yeah, I noticed."

"Now I bring you to the *sede*, then we have dinner."

"Looking after me tonight, and all!" said Vining, and he winked.

Maurizio telephoned me the following morning. "*Scusa: non ti disturbo?* Have you any idea what happened yesterday?"

"I got the impression that Bill wants to come to Rome."

"*Ah, sì?*"

"He liked the apartment, and Beppe seems to be showing him the city."

"But this is serious."

"Will you see him this morning?"

"*Perforza.* I must."

From that moment, it was as though he and Vining had disappeared. On Sunday, I published the news of Vining's trip to Rome; on Monday, I was telephoned by Gaudenzio. "Have you heard? Vining's not coming!"

"Are you sure?"

"*Ma sì, ma sì!*" I could almost see him at the other end of the telephone, hopping and shifting in his agitation. "It's in the London papers; we were telephoned by Valentini."

"Didn't he sign a 'compromise' while he was here?"

"*Ma che compromesso!* He'd given his word, everything was arranged; the President and I were flying to London tomorrow. We shall bring an action! We'll go to FIFA! I thought an Englishman's word was his bond!"

"Has he given any reason?"

"He's disappeared, Valentini can't find him; his club say they don't know anything. We'd shown him his apartment, he'd accepted terms, we'd settled the whole thing; what can have happened?"

"I've no idea."

I took the train to Milan that morning and found the city, as I always did, a pale, functional antidote to Rome. If Maurizio knew where I stayed in Rome, then I knew where he ate in Milan – at one of the innumerable *Trattorie Toscane*. He had been there, they told me, the previous evening. At half past eight I returned, and took a table. At ten minutes to nine, Maurizio appeared; he was with Vining. I called him, and he wheeled about in alarm.

"*Ma che! Ma cosa fai qui?* What are you doing here?"

"I came to see you."

"Following me around, eh?" Vining said, with calm good cheer.

"Well, you're a celebrated man."

"A *wanted* man, you mean; they was all looking for me in London, and now Maurizio says they're all looking for me in Rome."

They joined me for dinner, Maurizio full of a nervous, hunted amiability.

"Have you signed?" I asked Vining, and he gave a quick, questioning glance at Maurizio.

"Tomorrow," said Maurizio, in English, "but is all very secret."

"You won't write nothing, will you, Brian?" Vining said.

"Nothing before Sunday."

"I think by Sunday will be all right," Maurizio said.

"What changed your mind, Bill?"

"We-ell… I mean, you got to choose the best offer," he said, in that tone of worldly resignation so strange in anyone so young. "You got to do the best for yourself, ain't you?"

"I think it's *better* playing here in Milan," Maurizio said. "Yeah, well, I mean, that's another point, too."

And if Trastevere make a better offer still? I thought, but said nothing. For it seemed that the serial could last indefinitely, point and counterpoint, offer and counter-offer, while Vining swayed between the two great cities like a pendulum.

I left Milan the following afternoon; Maurizio, in the meanwhile, had telephoned me three times. "You won't write anything? You won't publish it until I tell you? You won't mention it to anybody? You'll be first to have the news, I swear!"

"Maurizio, I must say *something* about it on Sunday."

"Then I'll telephone you, I'll 'phone you at your home, on Thursday night."

When I came back to London, it was to find two Italcables from Gaudenzio, three 'phone messages from Valentini, two from Jack Collins. The following morning was a crazy counterpoint of voices; voices angry, voices agonized, voices plaintive and incredulous; Gaudenzio's voice, Valentini's voice, Collins' voice. "*Ma un inglese, come puo comportarsi in una maniera simile?*... I've told Joe Withington, I've told him that I mean it... but have you seen him? Where is he?... Where?... Where?... Where?"

I stayed at home on Thursday evening, but Maurizio did not telephone. The daily papers were full of headlines such as :

BILLY VINING DISAPPEARS
ENGLAND STAR VANISHES
WE DON'T KNOW WHERE HE IS,
SAY TRASTEVERE

On Sunday, untramelled by Maurizio, I was able to explode my bomb; Vining was in Milan.

That evening, I had Maurizio's sad, low monotone on the telephone once more.

"Where are you, Maurizio?"

"I'm in London."

"And everything's fixed?"

"*Be*'! I think so."

"What if Trastevere increase *their* offer?"

"We've told him that we'll still offer more."

"Has he actually signed the contract?"

"We sign tomorrow, then I fly back to Milan, with the President. Come to the Rovers' ground in the morning; we're giving a Press Conference for the signing."

"Will Valentini be there?"

"*Non credo,*" said Maurizio, with a giggle.

The Rovers' ground lay in the East End, a flower of the narrow, sombre streets, lying a mile away from Dockland; a monument of dull red, corrugated iron. Several photographers and journalists were already standing inside the carpeted main entrance, while a television van was drawn up outside.

Withington appeared through a door with a mottled glass panel; he seemed tense and tired.

"So it's over at last," I said, drawing him aside.

"I'll be glad when it is, mate," he answered me, wearily. "What with Italians screaming at me every day from *their* end, this madman Collins over here, and the kid changing his mind every other day, they've just about driven me crackers between them."

"He's here, is he?"

"No, he hasn't arrived yet. The Italian fellow's meant to be bringing him."

There was a small commotion at the door, and Maurizio came in, shepherding a little, desiccated man in a dark brown suit, and a high, brown Homburg."

"The President," Maurizio, anxiously presented him to me, "*il commendator Celio.*"

"I thought you were bringing Bill with you," Withington said.

"Yes! We arrive at his house, but he'd left. I think he's coming on his own."

"Well there's no point in waiting down here, then. We might as well all wait in the boardroom." And Withington led the way upstairs; the little boardroom already glowed with the cruel, incandescent glare of a television lamp. Men in shirtsleeves were responding to the calls of a shirtsleeved director. "Bloody television," a journalist said, behind me. "We'll be kept mucking about here till lunchtime."

We sat down here and there about the room. On the long, oval table lay blotting paper, Biro pens, and several small white piles of paper. Three of the club directors arrived, and Withington escorted them to their places at the table, together with Maurizio and the President.

"All we want now is the star, eh, Joe?" a journalist said.

A quarter of an hour passed, twenty minutes. Cigarette smoke curled in the air, the club secretary poured us beer and whisky.

"Ring him, Stan," Withington told him, but the secretary returned to say, "His mother says she thought he's on his way here."

Half an hour had gone. I looked at Maurizio; he was talking, with pale urgency, to the President. "We'll give him ten more minutes," Withington said.

Then, from below, came the sound of a high, squeaky voice protesting, "You can't stop me! I've *got* to go in! It's vital!" A dozen heads turned, Withington's among them, his brown face set and suspicious. There was a ponderous thumping of feet on the stairs, and at last Jack Collins appeared, pink and breathless, in the doorway.

"What do you want?" Withington said. "I thought I told you to stay away from this club."

"I've got a message," Collins said.

"*What* message?"

But Collins stood his ground, as though fortified by a deep certainty that the moment was his. There was silence in the room, while he seemed to be gathering breath poising himself for a pronouncement; I found myself looking, incongruously, at his great black boots. A television camera began to whirr like the feathers of a ptarmigan, and Withington snapped, "You can turn *that* thing off."

Then Collins spoke, high and fluting. "Gentlemen, I've just left Billy Vining. He's asked me to come here and say that he intends to stay in England."

There was immediate commotion, a great chorus of wonder and interrogation. Above it, Withington's voice rose, "What do you mean? *You've* got nothing to do with it! You're not his agent!"

"I am," said Collins, clearing his throat and looking at the ceiling. "He's come back to me for my advice."

"What did he say, Jack?" someone asked. The notebooks were out. A microphone on a cord was thrust by someone before Collins' great, setting sun of a face.

"He wasn't happy out there," Collins said. "He decided that he didn't like it... the language... the food... everybody speaking Italian. He's only a young boy... it was all very, very strange to him... and his mother couldn't have gone with him... she'd have had to stay in England." Question, exclamation, more questions. Beside me, Maurizio was gripping my arm in his despair. "But is it *possible*?" his sad voice moaned. "How can one explain it? It's ridiculous! It's inconceivable!"

Beside him, the President's face had now grown Sphinx-like in its dull dismay.

"It's better in Italy! " Maurizio said, and now his tone was almost coaxing, his sad face came closer against mine, as the journalists swarmed round Collins, leaving the three of us apart. "Admit it; it's better in Italy! The people are so much nicer! The people are more *sincere!*"

The director's wife

I hated the place from the moment I got up there; it was a miserable little town, you couldn't do nothing except go to the pictures. I'd never have moved up there at all, I'd have trained in London, only part of the offer was this job in a paint factory, which more or less meant ten quid a week extra, for nothing. On top of that, I got fifteen from the club, so altogether I was making more going outside the League than what I would have done if I'd stayed in the First Division. There wasn't no fun in the football, though, clump and bang and *marking* all the time; some of them marked you so close I reckoned the two of you would of been better off leaving the field and sitting in the lavatory, the whole game. And if you put through a real good ball, they'd make it into a bad one, because they was always so slow anticipating, and then the crowd would give you the bird. It was marvellous.

On top of that, I knew I was still good enough for the First Division, only when United put me on the list, see, I felt choked about it; I thought, right, if you think you're chucking me out, after all I done for you, you ain't getting no fee for it, anyway. If a non-League club makes me a good offer, go, so when it come, I did.

The week before the season started, they had a club social, and all the players was expected to attend; it was the supporters that was keeping the club going, they was putting in a hundred quid a week. Anyhow, that was where I met her the first time, her husband had brought her, he was Vice-Chairman. I'd seen him before, and I didn't like him; sort of a red baby face and a little moustache, one of them that thought he could throw his weight about because he was a builder, and he'd made a bit of money. He says, "Barker, I want you to meet my wife," and she takes my hand, and instead of letting it go, she was squeezing it, and she brought it all the way down, very slow, right down close to the front of her dress, until she was practically holding it against her twot, and all the time, you know, she's looking at me, right in the eyes, and I'm wondering, what's all this, then?

But her husband, Manners, he didn't seem to notice nothing; just stood there looking on, so I said, "Can I have this dance, then?" and we went out on to the floor. Dancing with her she was even worse, pressing herself right up close against you, and I was getting embarrassed, because every time we went round I could see him standing there watching us, and I thought, what's she trying to do, what's she up to? I looked at him, but you couldn't tell what he was thinking, he never seemed to have no expression, just those small little eyes, like a pig's they were, staring.

She said, "Are you going to get lots of goals for us?" only the way she said it was like it wasn't what she meant; she was *breathing* it at me. She wasn't bad, either, a bit on the fat side, but she'd got a nice figure, and she was blonde, but you could see it come out of the old bottle. I reckoned she was younger than what he was, in her thirties, and he couldn't have been less than forty, looking at him.

I turned up at the ground for training the next Monday evening, and one or two of the boys was having a bit of a go at me. One of them says, "It ain't taken him long," and another one says, "You mean it ain't taken her long." I said, "What are you on about?" making like I didn't know; then Len Challis, the captain, he was centre-half, says, "I'd keep a look-out, me old mate, if I was you; if you want to stay here, that is."

"I don't care if I stay here or not," I says.

"Well," he says, "that's your affair then, ain't it?" and they didn't say no more. Out on the field, though, I was doing a bit of ball practice with our left winger, Sammy Scott, and I says to him, "What are they all on about, then? She come right at me, she grabbed hold of me hand like she was never going to let go."

"That's right," he says, "that's what she does to everybody."

"Well, has she done it to you?" I says.

"Yes," he says, "she's done it to everybody."

"Well, has everybody had a go at her, then?"

"No," he says, "it's dangerous, everyone's careful. After she's done it, she tells."

"What, tells him?" I says, "her old man?" and he says, "That's right, Billy Rose was screwing her last season, the right winger; they went and cancelled his contract."

"Well, I don't care what they do with me," I said, " they can cancel it or they can stuff it," because I knew one thing, anyway; Billy Rose hadn't got no England cap.

Anyhow, I didn't think no more about it for a time; I didn't see nothing of her till after we'd played the second match, it was a mid-week match at home, against Gloucester. We won it 2-1, I got them both, and in the board room afterwards she took my hand, like she done before, and she said, "Why haven't you come to see me?" and I says, "You never asked me," and she says, "I don't have to ask you," and she was blinking her eyes and all and putting on the same voice she had before, and I didn't like it, because it, was right in the middle of everybody, in public, so I said, "All right I'll phone you, then," and I went away.

The next time I was at the ground, Joe Lumley, the manager, called me into his office and said,"There's been criticism about your play."

"Well,"I said, "thank you very much; that's marvellous, ain't it? We win the match, I get both goals, and people already start knocking me." He wasn't too happy about it himself, I could see that. Him and I got on okay, because he was a decent bloke, Joe; we'd played against one another when he was with Pompey.

"It's not me, Charlie," he says, "it's one or two of the directors, you know what these Boards are like, in a little town."

"Well, which ones?" I says, "and what criticisms have they got? You tell me, and I'll have it out with them."

"They say you're holding the ball too long," he says. "They say it might be all right in the First Division, but it don't work in this class of football."

Well that choked me, I can tell you. "You can tell them from me they're a lot of bloody twots," I says. "The only reason I'm holding it is because no one ain't moving into position. In the First Division you don't *need* to hold it that long; people are moving."

"I know that," he says, "but you know what it's like, Charlie; directors. They got a few simple little ideas in their head, and you can't tell them nothing different; it's too complicated for them."

"You still haven't told me which ones," I says.

"I'll tell you," he says, "if you promise me you won't say nothing to them. One's the Chairman, and the other's Manners."

"Oh, him? " I says, "I reckon I know why, and all; it's that bloody cow of a wife of his. I can't help it if she keeps on sorting me out."

"Look, Charlie," he says, "I know it's difficult, but you got to keep away from her."

"Me?" I says. "You tell *her* to keep away from me."

"I can't," he says, "Manners has put more money into the club than anyone bar the Chairman and the supporters. I know it ain't fair on you, but if I can't say nothing to her, I got to say something to you, haven't I?"

A few days later, she rings me up. I was in lodgings there, and I hated it. "Hallo," she says, "you're a nice one. I thought you was going to get in touch with me."

"Was I?" I says. "I don't remember nothing about it." There was some music playing in the background, and she was talking like she was half asleep, all sort of come-and-get-it, even more than she had at the match.

"Guess what I'm doing," she says, and I said, "I don't know, I don't know what you're doing."

"I'm lying on the bed," she says, "and I'm naked. Do you want to come over and see me?"

Well, what could you say? I hadn't had no crumpet since I'd been there. I sort of half remembered what Joe had told me at the ground, about her telling, but at times like that you don't really think, you sort of get carried away. "You're sure you're not kidding?" I says, because I was thinking, she sounds like a nut case, only a nut case would say a thing like that, but she says, "No, come over, come over."

I took a taxi, and when I got there, she opened the door in her dressing-gown. She took my hand, and she pulled it right down between her tits then she said, "Come upstairs," and I didn't need no asking twice. I followed her upstairs and into the bedroom, and she took her dressing-gown right off – she wasn't wearing nothing underneath it – and I give it to her on the bed. It was all right, too, and all.

When we'd finished, and we was lying there, I says, "Do you do this sort of thing often, then, ringing people up and telling them you ain't got nothing on?" and she says, "Only with people I like, like you."

Then I remembered again what I'd heard about her telling her husband and I says, "What about your old man, then, what if he finds out?" and she says, "I don't mind him, he's no good to me."

"Well, I mind," I says, "because I reckon he's got wind of something already."

"Don't you worry, darling," she says, "he won't find out; he's just suspicious, he's jealous of everybody, he hates me even talking to anyone."

"There must be something in it," I said, "because he's trying to sort me out already, him and that bloody Chairman, after just a couple of games."

"Oh, that's just Ted," she says, "he always has to criticise, and what he says, the Chairman follows."

"Well, that makes it worse," I says, "if he's stirred it all up. Them two, they know as much about football as my bloody arse does." I could just see his face then, like a bloody pink balloon, them little eyes and the little tiny moustache, and I thought, what bleeding right has he got, telling *me* how to play? And then I screwed her again, and I felt better after that, but then I started looking round the room, the carpets and the mirrors and the wardrobes and all, and I thought, why should *he* have a bloody house like this and give me orders, just because he's been able to fiddle himself a few building deals?

But when I got home, I started worrying about what I done, and the more I thought about it, the more I thought about how she'd rung up, and some of the things she'd said, the more I reckoned she must be a nut case.

I'd said I'd go in and see her the next afternoon – it was easy getting away from the factory, the boss there didn't really care if I was there or not – but I thought I better scrub round it. Then, when the time come round, I thought, well, might as well be hung for a sheep as for a lamb, if she'd tell him about twice she'd tell him about once, so what was the difference? And anyway, I knew what women was like, if I did turn it in, she'd probably tell him out of spite.

So I went there again, and it was okay, too, except this time I looked around the house a bit, and I was thinking again, what the hell has that fat bastard done to have a place like this? As for her, it was okay while I was screwing her, but in between she was asking me all sorts of questions, not just did I love her? which was what I expected, but had I got any other girls, had I met any here in the town, had I left one behind in London, and were they as good as she was, questions like that. It got on me nerves, after a while.

That Saturday, we was away to Cheltenham, and she and her husband come in the team coach. I'm not kidding, she was crazy, she was going past me, on to the coach, and as she went past, she grabbed hold of me – he couldn't have been more than a couple of yards in front of her. One of the lads looked at me and he says, "What are *you* going so red about, Charlie?" and I just had to try and laugh it off, I'd like to of killed her.

On the coach, she'd managed to get rid of her husband, he was sitting behind the Chairman, and she'd got an empty seat beside her; when I went past, she was bloody well patting it, but I made out like I hadn't noticed. All the way there I was scared stiff she was going to come and start talking to me, but she never got up. Still, by the time we arrived I didn't feel much like playing, and I had a bad game, I don't mind admitting it.

That Monday, Joe had me in the office again. "You know what it is, Charlie," he says.

"Yeah," I says, "I suppose the two of them have been carrying on again. Well, all right, I had a bad game, I'm not denying it."

"What went wrong?" he says. He looked more worried than what I did.

"Nothing," I says, "it happens to everyone, don't it, bad games? You got to have one now and again."

"Yeah, but it makes it difficult," he says, "coming as early as this; it gives them an excuse. Old Manners never wanted to bring you here in the first place, he said it was costing the club too much money. The Chairman wasn't sure, and in the end he went with the majority."

"All right, I'll go," I said, "I'll go, if that's how they feel.

"Look, Charlie," he says, "don't be like that, I'm not asking you to go, I want you to stay. I've just got to find out what's the matter; all the way to the match you looked like something was on your mind."

"No," I said, "there wasn't nothing on me mind. I told you, I just had a bad game. When it don't run, it don't run."

"It's not her," he says, "is it? Mrs Manners? It's not her that's upsetting you? She hasn't been going on at you, has she?"

"What, her?" I says. "I told her to bugger off." But the next time I see Manners, he seemed to be looking at me very old fashioned like, and in the end, when I see her, I says to her, "You sure he don't know?"

"Of course he don't," she says.

"You sure you ain't told him?" I says, and she says, "The idea! What a thing to say!"

"Well you lay off that lark you was on right outside the bus," I says, "or I'll bloody well finish with you. In front of everyone, and all. It put me right off me game, I was worried all the time what the hell you was going to get up to next, and he don't need no excuse to have a go at me. He'll knock me when I've played good let alone when I've played bad. Old Joe told me he was against me coming here in the first place."

"That's 'cause he's jealous," she says, "he's jealous of anyone what's bigger than he is. Don't you take no notice of him."

The next game or two I did better, I was playing it more to their style, slowing it down so they got time to cotton on to what I was doing, then giving them square balls they could get out of trouble with by themselves, so they looked the mugs, not me.

I was going up there to see her two or three times a week – she always used to say it was quite all right, nobody wouldn't come near us the times she picked – and one way and another, I wasn't finding it so bad. Good money, crumpet whenever you wanted it – and all for nothing. I still used to think of him when I went up there to screw her; the way he'd been knocking me behind me back, the way he'd tried to stop me coming there, the way he ponced around the place like he was king of the bloody castle. So when he looked at me, I used to look straight back at him.

"Hullo, Barker," he used to say, out of the corner of his mouth, like he only talked to you because he had to, and I'd say, "Hullo, Manners," dead serious. "Thought you had quite a good game today," he'd say, and I'd say, "Did you, me old cock? I say, that's terribly decent of you," and he didn't know how to take it. But he never said nothing, so I reckoned what he give me was just *looks*: he didn't know nothing definite.

Now and again one of the boys would say, "Getting on all right with Mrs Manners, Charlie? Giving you what you want, is she?" and I'd laugh it off, like, I'd say, "Course she is," or, "What do *you* think, mate?"

"Ain't got eyes for no one else now, has she?" Len Challis said, and I says, "Course she ain't, I'm the handsome one," but next time I saw her, I told her to keep away from me, when there was people.

I used to get up to the house about four o'clock, and I'd stay till six, because half past six was the time she expected him home. One afternoon I was getting off the bed, getting ready to go, and she said, "Don't go yet," and I said, "What, and let him find me here? What do you think I am? "

"No," she says, "we got nothing to worry about, he's gone off to Banbury to see a contractor, he won't be back till late. You can stay."

"You sure?" I said, because this was the first time I'd ever been as late as this, but she said yes, of course she was sure, so I got back on the bed, and I give it her again.

Round about half past six, we was right in the middle of it all when I thought I heard something down below, and I says, "What's that? You hear that?" but she says, "Hear what? I didn't hear nothing."

I said, "It sounded like the front door," and she says, "It couldn't have been. I told you, he's in Banbury."

The next moment, there's footsteps coming up the stairs, and I says, "I'm right, he bloody well is back; where can I go?"

But she just sat up there like she wasn't worried, just like she was, didn't bother to put no clothes on or nothing, and she says, "It'll be all right, leave it to me," and I said, "You fucking knew it, didn't you? You knew he was coming back," and I belted over to lock the door, but there wasn't no key in it, and I says, "Where's the key," and she says, "There ain't one," and she'd started lighting a cigarette. Next moment he had the door open and he'd caught me standing there bollock naked, and she's sitting on the bed and smoking.

He looks at us and he says to me, "What the hell are *you* doing here?" and I says, "You'd better ask *her*, hadn't you?" and she looks at him, all calm, and she says, "If you will keep bursting in on people, what do you expect?" Then they just kept looking at each other, him going redder and redder, like he was going to blow up, and her just smoking like she couldn't care less.

While they was doing that, I got across the room and got me trousers on, and then he started shouting at me, "Fuck off! Get out of my house! Go on, get out of it!" and she says, "I invited him here, and I'll tell him when he can leave," and he says, "You can both leave! You can get out together!" and she says, "You know you don't mean that." I'd never seen nothing like it; any minute he looked like he was going to cry.

Anyhow, I didn't need no telling twice; I grabbed up all me other clothes and I belted downstairs, putting them on while I went. They was still going on at each other when I got to the door; she was shouting as well, now, and I jumped on to a bus and all the way home, all I could think of was the way she'd let me in for it, because I knew she had, I knew it was deliberate. *He* hadn't come back early or nothing, he hadn't been to Banbury at all.

I didn't sleep too good that night, I don't mind telling you, what with wondering what was going to happen to me now. He'd kick me out of the club, that was dead certain, and on top of that I could find meself in court, and paying Christ knows how much costs and all.

There was a phone call for me about ten o'clock, and I knew it was her, but I wouldn't take it, I told them to say I'd gone out. Next morning she phoned me again, and I said I was out again, then she phoned me at the factory, and this time I bloody well had to take it, or they might get nosy. She said, "I'm sorry about last night," and I said, "You ought to be," and she said, "Honest, I didn't know he was going to be back so quick," and I said, "What do you take me for?" and I hung up on her. Then she went and wrote to me – how it wasn't her fault and she didn't know and she was sorry, but I never answered her, I just burnt it, so no one wouldn't find it.

I was waiting for something to happen, for Joe to say he wanted a word with me, or something, but nothing did. When Saturday come round, it was still on me mind, wondering how they was going to behave and all, the two of them, but they never turned up. I still had a bad game, though, even though I scored a goal and we won.

On the Tuesday afternoon I come in for the training and Len Challis says, "Have you heard what's happened?" and I says, "No," and he says, "Manners has resigned," and I says, "Why?" I says, because I couldn't make no sense out of it, I was still worried, and he says, "I don't know, he didn't give no reasons. Probably wants to keep his old woman away from the team, I shouldn't wonder."

Well, I couldn't believe me ears, but later on I spoke to Joe as well, and he confirmed it, it was true; and I thought, blimey, I'm dead lucky, dead lucky, because it could so easy have gone the other way.

A day or two later, one of the other lads comes up to me and says, "You heard the story that's going round about Manners, ain't you; why's he's resigned? They say he caught his old woman having a go with one of us players; it wasn't you, was it, Charlie?"

"What me?" I says, "I don't know where all this story started, just because I chatted her up a few times at dances and that."

I only saw her again once, it must have been in February; I was walking through the market square and somebody tooted their horn and it was her, she was parking her car. But I went by like I hadn't noticed.

Greenberg

Loyal and skeletal, Greenberg appeared one day in the United press-box, the latest of Freeman's friends. These were the early fifties, when there was still residual hope that Freeman would one day be rich, be famous, be all the things he'd promised to be, and knew he should be.

Kind and cocksure, with his puns, his spectacles, his trilby hat – but over forty, now – he covered games for the Dispatch, and brought his friends, who had no right to be there. Of these, Greenberg, though so silent, was the most noticeable yet. He was very tall, unfailingly intense, given to long, fawn, shapeless raincoats, which he wore like shrouds; to a brown, high-crowned hat, worn without fantasy, flush on the crown of his head, where Freeman's trilby swooped like a kestrel. He never smiled. His eyes, small and myopic, behind tortoiseshell spectacles, were brown; the eyes of a sad, old dog.

When Freeman talked, he listened, as if listening were an active function. The tension of his thin body, the very inclination of his head, proclaimed: I'm listening, look at me, and you should listen, too. Later, as he gradually relaxed, he went one further, took to nodding; later still, to murmured choruses: "Joe's right, you know."

One saw him only at the two North London grounds, United and Rovers; perhaps because Freeman's writ ran no further, perhaps because he himself had a sense of the appropriate. For he was all North London, its quintessence, the distillation of its fogs, its ugly streets and shopping arcades, its multiple stores, its drab semi-detacheds. It was impossible to picture him in the country, unless it were in the middle of some field; a straggling, urban scarecrow. God knows what he did for a living; one imagined him travelling in ladies' garments, dealing in ugly furniture, doing something honest and dim, modestly rewarding, without prospects.

"Him?" said Freeman, oblivious throughout of the signs of growing independence, the first, faint rumblings of self-determination, "Stoke Newington, I think he lives. Or Stamford Hill." It was as if he, too, granted Greenberg no existence beyond the press-box, no ambitions that were not discipular. "Joe's right. If they'd listened to Joe... Joe knows the game."

Quixote and Panza, I thought, watching them one day from behind as they moved across the grey waste of the United car park, Greenberg adapting his long, gaunt strides to match the shorter, chirpier gait of Freeman, as he loomed above him. Yet which, on second thoughts, was Quixote, which Sancho Panza? Freeman, certainly, would have no doubts; he saw himself as a crusader. "The top soccer controversialist of our day," he had called himself, in the publicity hand-out for his latest enterprise, "Football Programmes International."

"Wonderful," said Greenberg who, in his second press-box season, had more to say. "A wonderful idea of Joe's. A man in Rio wants to collect Arsenal programmes, so now he can do it."

But the scheme, like all Freeman's schemes, had collapsed; other countries, for the most part, didn't issue programmes. "But if they *had*," cried Greenberg. "What a wonderful idea!"

Our conversations, those we had, took place in the car park, or in the tiny, crowded press-rooms at Rovers and United, over saucerless white cups of thick, undrinkable tea, over cheese and Spam sandwiches, over the occasional prize of a small cake. Around us, other journalists shoved and bustled in their lemming rush towards the tea urn. Elbows challenged one's cup of tea, feet ground into one's toes; Greenberg towered above the ruck like an ostrich, his Adam's apple bobbing with emotion. "Ronnie Klein," he'd say, naming an editor who once published Freeman in his short-lived magazine. "It went to his head. Ten-guinea shirts. Fifty-guinea suits. And telling *Joe* what to do ! *Joe!*"

Slowly, then, he was taking on a life of his own, though one noticed it only in retrospect. To talk at all was the first step, the next, to talk when Freeman was not beside him, like a puppeteer, even if Freeman was still almost always his subject.

The time came, though, when Freeman was not; instead, the subject was his nephews. Both were doing very well, and one guessed he couldn't be married, had perennially resigned himself to the status of admiring uncle. One nephew was a brilliant boy, 17 – "he's going to sit a scholarship to Cambridge." The other was younger, 14 – "not a student, he'll never make a student, but a natural footballer. I watch all his school games, Saturday mornings, before I come on here. This morning: what a goal! Left-footed! I only wish you'd been there to see it!"

Faithful and opaque, Freeman took him for granted. Freeman noticed nothing, continuing to make bad puns, cheerfully lay down the law, deplore his bad luck in the past: "And it was all fixed! The job was mine!" Greenberg, like the rest, had his function – that of Chorus – in return for which he saw the match for nothing. But Greenberg wasn't like the rest.

Next season, his third in the press-boxes, one suddenly became aware he had cut adrift. There he was, one autumn afternoon at Rovers, high up in the back row, sitting by himself; or rather, sitting between two reporters, neither of whom was Freeman. The same hat perched incongruously on his head, he blinked out over the field through the same spectacles. Baffled, I looked round for Freeman and at last saw him, rows and rows away, far down across the gangway; itself a frontier. Had they quarrelled, I wondered? Had Panza seen through Quixote, Quixote been disappointed in Panza? But in that case, why was Greenberg still there? Over the years, Choruses had come, been used, and had departed; interchangeable, replaceable.

At half-time in the press-room, where the steam of tea mingled with the steam of soaking raincoats, they did not speak to one another. In the case of Greenberg, gaunt and opaque, it might have meant anything or nothing, but there was something to the set of Freeman's back, turned consistently to Greenberg, which implied a huffy consciousness he was there.

It seemed to me, as the weeks went by and Greenberg changed with them, that Freeman increasingly took on the baffled aspect of a Frankenstein deserted by his monster.

In his next stage, Greenberg grew strangely interested in minutiae. It was guilt, perhaps, a lurking awareness that however long he haunted press-boxes, he had no right to be there. This, though he was always kind and patient with young journalists, sombrely welcoming, helping them decide just who had hit the post, which back had kicked off the line.

So, in this new phase, he came to care about attendance figures, about those little scraps of pasteboard passed along each row of journalists after half-time, bearing the number of spectators. "Did you get it?" he would ask, turning his anxious, sad, cadaverous face to the row behind him. "Forty-five thousand and what? Three-three-two. Thank you." And, relieved, he would write it down very carefully on his programme.

Then there were the goalscorers, or rather, not so much the goalscorers as the goal makers, pursued with almost genealogical zeal. "Who gave him the ball?" the hollowed face would turn to ask.

"Lewis."

"No, not him. The pass before that."

I never saw him with his hat off, nor his macintosh, even when spring came and the brighter days, when the sun shone on the United car park, as on a desert, gleamed – if you walked down the hill – from the glassy sides of Rovers' towering stands. If he did take the hat off he'd be bald, I knew; would have to be bald, his skull a vast egg, crossed by a few adventurous strands. One almost felt he had been born bald, been born wearing the hat, although beneath the brim of it, hair grew in bushy irrelevance down the back of his neck.

"My nephew," he said, one day at Rovers, when I met him walking up the wretched street from the Tube. "The brilliant one...?" I began, then changed it to "the Cambridge one?"

"No, no," he said, "that's not till Christmas, not the scholarship. The other one."

"The footballer?"

"That's right. I've talked to Johnny Wilkinson." This was the United manager, a silent man with a thick, red neck who sat, anguished, in the back row of the directors' box, suffering each mistake, identifying with each kick. From the press-box, right behind him, one could almost tell the state of a game, simply by looking at his neck.

"That's good," I said.

"He's interested. He'll send a scout."

"That's marvellous."

Often, now, he would be in the press-box when Freeman wasn't, suggesting total independence, access to passes of his own. And he grew more and more assertive, no longer craning on the edge of groups like an apologetic giraffe. Nor did he merely participate; he would contradict, interrupt, quite impervious; spluttering his disagreement, intruding in a sudden welter of words. "Yes, but that's not the point... it isn't... I mean, a man like that, a centre-forward, he's entitled to score goals."

Now he *was* Quixote, tilting at shibboleths, at self-styled lions of Fleet Street. "What about Dimmock?" he once cried, when a group of us one day were listening to a monologue, by a lion, on the failings of managers. The lion turned, ready to devour him, then said nothing. Greenberg, all bone and gristle, could plainly never be devoured. "A man like Dimmock," he said, his cavernous face drawn tighter than ever by the violence of his sincerity. "Where do you ever see an outside-left like him? I was a boy. My father took me."

In the New Year, he said to me, "My nephew. You remind me of him," and I said, confused, "The one who may turn pro?"

"No, no," he said, "the brilliant one. The Cambridge one. He's going there. He got his scholarship." "That's wonderful," I said.

"In Science," he said. "Natural Science. His headmaster at the school said they've never had a boy like that. Believe me, he'll end up as one of those... those nuclear..."

"Physicists," I heard myself say.

"That or the other thing. The rockets." "You must be very proud of him."

"I am," he said, "I am," and I remembered how he'd once been proud of Freeman.

Freeman never spoke to him, nor of him, and intrigued as I was, I could not bring myself to mention him to Freeman, greyer and less jaunty with the years, his jokes feebler, his ambitions no longer advertised. Once only in conversation did I mention Freeman's name to Greenberg, half experimentally. "Spoiled himself," said Greenberg, in a perfunctory mutter. "He spoiled himself, Joe." It sounded like an obituary.

Next August, when the evening games began, Greenberg brought his nephew, the Cambridge one, brought him into the press-box: "My nephew; he's going to Cambridge." The nephew was quite a good-looking boy, with a soft, full face, and wavy black hair; tall, though not as tall as Greenberg. He was modest, polite, and he seemed unembarrassed; perhaps, over the years of promise and fulfilment, he had grown used to his uncle's fulsomeness.

"You two," said Greenberg, introducing us. "You'd have a lot in common." I thought, wrongly and wonderingly, that the wheel had come full circle; Greenberg, an interloper in the press-box, was now bringing guests of his own.

But I was wrong. One windy afternoon at United, squeezed between a parked Bentley and a parked Jaguar, I saw him in tense conversation with one of the United directors; though all Greenberg's conversations were tense.

The director, like every United director, had about him the prosaic, suspicious air of a successful grocer, uneasy beyond the safety of his counter. He looked up at the gaunt, wobbling, talking head on its long, thin neck with a wondering wariness of which Greenberg seemed quite unconscious. They – or Greenberg – were talking, I supposed, of the other nephew, the footballer, of whom one still heard from time to time; he was having a trial with Finchley, the amateurs; he was "going to sign forms" for United, amateur forms; "his father wants him in the business."

Six weeks later, when next I covered a United game, Greenberg was in the directors' box. At first I could not believe it, was sure I had mistaken the front row of the press-box for the back row of the directors' box. But I hadn't. The narrow, bony, rain-coated shoulders, the irrelevant fringe of hair beneath the hat, sat, indeed, in the back row of the directors' box, five places down from Johnny Wilkinson, the manager.

Looking round for someone to discuss it with, I saw, in a corner of the press-box, Freeman; he, in turn, looking at the hat, the scraggy neck, with a thin, wounded smile.

During the match, I noticed that Greenberg's behaviour in the directors' box did not vary; he still, when a goal was scored, spoke anxiously to those around him, making notes on his programme, though he did not speak to the journalists behind him. At half-time, in the tea-room, Freeman's eyes met mine. "*Chuzpah*," he said. "You know what *chuzpah* means? The Jewish boy who shot his father and mother then said don't hang me, I'm an orphan."

I nodded, though I saw it differently. *Chuzpah* meant cheek and bounce, effrontery, and where was Greenberg's?

A month later, I saw him in the directors' box again, his nephew – the brilliant one – beside him. Now, when we met, he was still cordial in his taut, unrelated way, but there were modulations; a hint that he was privy to secrets. There were times, when he talked about United, that he said "we". "If we get a couple of quick goals... that was never a goal, that one; they robbed us." The club, it almost seemed, had taken the place once filled by Freeman: "the best in England, greatest players, greatest manager. You know our trouble? We play *too much* football."

January, with its fogs and cup ties, its sheets of grey, heavy rain assailing the bleak stadium, gave way to February, to March, to spring, the Cup Final, and the terminal evening games; the pitches brown and grassless, mud flats with a fringe of green. Then it was summer, and hiatus; foreign tours, transfers, practice matches; a process as regular as the seasons themselves.

United opened the new championship with a home match, which I went to report. Inside the car park, Freeman met me. "*Ha*-llo, Brian. Heard the one about the two Jewish hair-dressers?" I listened, tried to laugh, then I saw Greenberg, getting out of a Daimler, the vice-chairman's Daimler, still awkward as an ostrich. Raincoated as always, he stood for a moment in the sunshine, there in the middle of the car park, peering dimly round. Yet there was something in the stance of the absurd, thin body, something in the poise of the head on its meagre neck, which suggested he was not looking for people, but rather looking round a new domain.

It was only when his gaze reached Freeman that it paused, then fell and, clumsily, he turned away.

"Didn't you know?" asked Freeman, as we watched the tall, stooped figure moving with the vice-chairman towards the officials' entrance. His right hand held a programme out to me, thumb agitating on the front cover, and there, beneath the pyramid of directors' names, I saw the new one: L. B. Greenberg.

The footballers

"H A L L O-my-dear!" Franco never spoke on the telephone, he bellowed; a great lion's roar suggesting his scepticism that the instrument really transcended distance.

"Listen! This morning you come down with me to Rifredi: I make you see what I am doing! Lovely boys! Beautiful players! You have no idea! Just like young English players: you will see!"

It was the highest compliment he could pay, based on a strange Anglophilia which derived solely from his admiration for English football. I myself was a lucky beneficiary; friendship, goodwill, generosity rained down upon me, as on the son of some deceased national hero.

"I'll be delighted to come," I told him, in Italian, but Franco boomed back at me in his curious sing-song English, at once fluent and grotesque, a switchback of mistaken cadences, odd transliterations. "Very well! I see you at ten, in Cathedral Square." There were times when he went too far.

It was a clear, pale day in late October; the sun shone bright and heatless out of a God the Father sky, full of billowing cloud. Above the city, seen from my window, the villas of Fiesole stood out sharp and deceptively close from their dark green mounting of cyprus. Down river, the trees in the Cascine were less luxuriant now, and the Arno itself moved slow, on one of its ugly, khaki days.

Franco wasn't in the Piazza del Duomo at ten, but then I had not expected him to be. He was always late and seldom in haste, arriving at last with a casual, muttered apology. With its great, swelling dome, its garish red, white and green walls, the Duomo towered above the square in vulgar majesty, like a handsome woman in tawdry clothes. Outside the large bar, which was one of Franco's rendezvous, my hand was seized by a friend of his, a season ticket holder at the football stadium, curly grey haired, with the contrasting face of a cherub.

"*Ciao caro! Prende un calle?*"

To know Franco was a magic passport; previously this man had shown me only the detached hostility which the Florentine reserves for foreigners. I thanked him, and we went into the bar. "Waiting for Franco, eh?" he asked. I said that I was. He chuckled, as Franco's friends and pupils did when they talked about him, a chuckle of benign astonishment, shocked admiration; that of a parent with a loved, outrageous child. "*Ma che fenomeno,*" he said, shaking his head, "*che fenomeno.*" I agreed, and conversation flagged, until – the eternal last resort – we began to talk about La Fiorentina. But within minutes Franco himself had arrived – "Oh! My dear!" – great arms outstretched in a reflex gesture of delight and repentance, which dissolved at once as the arms dropped to his sides, and he turned to the three or four men who instantly surrounded him.

He radiated an intense, physical masculinity; a tall, outdoor man, vastly broad, his white shirt unbuttoned, despite the weather, to reveal his deep, bronzed chest. Over his shoulder, characteristically, he had slung his jacket, as though scornfully deferring to an ordinance of dress. His face still retained part of its summer tan, but the impression it gave was rather one of wind-whipped ruddiness. His nose was large and jagged, his chin strong, and his metallic blond hair was combed back thickly from his forehead.

The men eddied about him, waves around a rock, half mocking, half his disciples. "Eh, Franco!" they said, "What about the Fiorentina?" and looked at one another half giggling, like children, knowing each response. "*Macchè Fiorentina!*" Franco shouted, in the thick, rough Tuscan of the Florentine backstreets. "That team doesn't understand a – about football!" He perorated on without looking at them, louder and louder, as though reciting a set piece which nothing they might say could modify. Names of players, names of managers, were fed gleefully by them into the machine, and each in turn produced its roar of contemptuous abuse, larded with obscenity. The man with curly hair turned to me, rolled his eyes in apology, and said, "You know how he always exaggerates…"

"Who exaggerates?" Franco bellowed. "I tell you I've two boys in my team now who could…" But here his remarks were lost in a tumult of jeers and mock applause. Again, he seemed unaffected, neither angry nor amused; he merely raised his voice still higher and shouted, with the strange, aspirated Florentine "C", "*Sanno giohare, sanno giohare,*" they know how to play. Then he put a hand absently on my shoulder and guided me out of the bar, like a casual sheep dog.

We took the *filobus* from the Piazza del Duomo to the Industrial Zone. The journey began in Florence, in the shadow of the duomo; went by the fortifications, with their miniature lake, then passed speedily into No Man's

Land. The city's perimeter might have been anywhere, functional and shallow, a compound of ugly bypasses, garrisoned by numberless garish filling stations; of railway bridges, hurtling lorries, grey, anonymous side streets. We got out, fighting our way down the narrow aisle of the bus, at Rifredi, where Franco trained his young players. This was the Industrial Zone, and it had always seemed right to me that the football ground should lie among this waste of factory buildings, one storied, white walled; an ugly, half-hearted gesture at modernity. Industry and football belonged together, irrelevant alike to the nature of the city itself.

We walked into the little stadium. The stretch of grass – uncommon enough in Tuscany – was dark green and uneven, worn in front of the goals, at either end. Round it stood a fence of wire netting, a reminder of combustible passions. A small, compact grandstand with terraced blocks instead of seats stood apart as though abandoned there. Just outside the ground rose a workers' apartment block, a futuristic barracks, its outer stairways a maze of stone corkscrews, its terrace walls inlaid with shiny purple.

On the field, several boys in football kit were kicking a ball to one another, moving with the plasticity of the young Italian, and the young Italian's delight in his own virtuosity. They bounced the ball on their thighs, tried to flick it over their heads with their heels, or hurled themselves into the air in an attempted *rovesciata*, scissor-kicking backwards, high above their heads. Franco greeted them with an offhand cry of, "*Oh, ragazzi!*" and for the second time that morning he was surrounded – "*Senti, Franco... Franco!*" the boys asking him a score of eager questions.

Here, too, Franco moved with a strange detachment; gentler, now, eyes still distant, moving a hand now and then in a gesture of deprecation. Suddenly, with a bellow, he was wide awake, seizing a ball, calling for another, dividing the boys into groups, marshalling them with the abuse of a drill sergeant. "*Bischero! Testa di cazzo!* What are you doing, standing there playing with yourselves?"

The boys seemed unresentful. They responded, brisk and alert, to his commands, as though the mastering of each skill, each exercise, were of ritual importance. And indeed, it was; their very lives were in prospect; proficiency in this game could make the difference between wealth and unemployment, mean wages and a life of fast cars, new flats, women, adulation. Through Franco and his training lay the path to the rich professional clubs, backed by millionaires – themselves in search of that corrosive goal of the Italian male, the making of the *bella figura*. A few of these boys would succeed, some would have mediocre careers with lesser professional clubs, others would fall by the wayside, forced to abandon their dreams.

Franco, then, for all his four-square masculinity, was a trader in dreams, holding in this sport a unique position. He had a prospector's eye for latent talent, could find his players in the streets and squares, kicking a rubber ball, in minor matches, in obscure teams run by priests. Then he would train and coach them, give them money to subsist on, play them in his own, junior team, and hope to sell them at last to one of the rich professional clubs in deals of labyrinthine complexity.

Once, I tried to leave the little stadium, but Franco caught sight of me at once. "No, no! You must see my centre-'alf! Lovely player!" and reluctantly I stayed.

The centre-half was tall, graceful and feline, with a Grecian head and physique. Perhaps it was his very fluency and relaxation that made me remark, by contrast, another boy, heavier in build and movement, strained and alert, his thatch of fair hair resembling Franco's. If the centre-half received most of the praise and individual attention, this other player was obviously the butt. Franco abused them all from time to time, but the blond boy was more often the target than any of the others, while the abuse, now I paid attention, seemed sharper, and more sharply felt.

The consequence was inevitable: the boy tried too hard to do well, and accordingly did badly, the strong body tense, so that it resisted the ball, instead of yielding and persuading it. "You can't play!" Franco shouted at him, on one of these occasions. "How can anyone as ugly as you are be a footballer? With a face like yours, you're only good for scaring women!" There was sycophantic laughter at this, and from where I sat, the boy seemed almost to be in tears.

When Franco at last came off the field, and I strolled forward with relief to meet him, the boy was at his side, anxious and pleading. "But Franco, Franco, show me what I'm doing wrong! I know I haven't got it yet, but show me!" Franco did not turn to look at him, but merely growled, "I've shown you a dozen times." "But how can I improve? Tell me!" "You can't improve. You're an idiot."

"But *Franco!*" Now I could plainly see tears in his eyes. His face as Franco had said, was ugly, yet it was not displeasing. The jaw was long and heavy and blunt, like a trowel, the mouth hung slightly open, as though drawn down irresistibly by the weight below. Altogether the impression given was that of a friendly, clumsy dog, a Newfoundland puppy, desperately anxious to please.

"But Franco..." he said.

"I'll show you tomorrow," Franco told him, in blunt dismissal. The boy went in with the others to change, and I felt glad and relieved. Wanting to intervene, I had been held back by knowing I had no real part in the scene, that my very presence was no more than an accident. "Who is he?" I asked. Franco shrugged. "One of my players: Carlo Paolozzi. I find him in a street team when he was thirteen." "Is he good?"

Again a shrug: this time more a movement of the head than of the shoulders; the subject clearly did not touch him. "His ball control's quite good. He studies the game a lot. But he's too much of an idiot: you saw his face?" And here Franco gave a cruel parody of the boy, protruding his chin, opening his mouth, rolling his eyes.

We waited for the players to change, they emerged dressed in heavy woollen jerseys and cheap sports jackets, then together we made our way to the *filobus* stop. "What a woman!" Franco was saying now, while the boys nudged each other and guffawed with delight. "Three times I went with her, and she said to me, 'I've never come across a man like you. You're the strongest man I've ever known.'" "Bravo Franco!" said one of the boys. "But it's true!" Franco shouted, and his voice rose higher still. "I'll show her to you. Brothel stuff, *roba da casino, ma bella bella!*"

At the bus stop, the conversation returned to football. Franco began to expound tactics, to analyse the team's previous match, and Carlo, eyes shining with delight, spread his arms in a clumsy, touching gesture of joy and cried, "But Franco, you're great! *Tu sei grande!*"

Franco had invited me to lunch, and we left the bus a few hundred yards from the rough stone apartment house where his family lived, not far from Rifredi. He pressed the bell, a buzzer sounded, the door opened, and from high above, wafted faintly down the dark stair well, came a cry of, "*Chi e?*"

"It's me!" Franco shouted, and we began to ascend the endless stairs. As we climbed, he was no longer talking about his boys, of whom I'd expressed due admiration, but about English players. What did I think of Stanley Matthews? Had I ever seen Shackleton play? His knowledge of names and teams was astonishing, almost compulsive, the fruit of endless poring over a thousand books and magazines. "It's not the same in England," he said, nostalgically, with a smile that envied me my innocence. "In English football, there's *serieta.*"

His pale, thin, weary stepmother opened the door, and he gave her a cursory greeting. I tried to atone with a greater cordiality, knowing it was hopeless to try to change the pattern, to alter the facts of acceptance and defeat. I was Franco's friend, his appendage, and as such, she expected no more from me than she received from him. In the little dining room, with its glass-doored cabinet of china and its two worn, chintz covered armchairs, his father sat reading *l'Unita*: in his lap lay the plump black and white cat. As I came in, he put down the Communist newspaper and said, in rumbling Tuscan, "Well, then, what about the Americans?"

"I don't know," I said.

"Children," he answered, the old eyes full of gleeful malice, "all of them. But Stalin will take care of them, you'll see."

"Don't bother him with politics," Franco said, swinging out of the room again, to the bathroom.

"He's interested in politics," said the old man. "Only cretins aren't interested in politics."

When Franco had washed, he called me into his room to show me a magazine article. It was more of a cell than a room, gloomy, cramped and windowless, with a narrow bed hard up against one wall. Alongside it ran a bookshelf; I had looked at his curious collection of books many times while waiting for him to arrive. Several were about English football; there was a paperbacked copy of "The Constant Nymph", an English grammar, and a little platoon of pamphlets about sex. In that room, in its contents, its very physical dimensions, there seemed to be expressed the whole tragedy of the Italian male.

In the dining-room, the bowls of *pastina in brodo* were already cooling on the table. Franco ate quickly and singlemindedly, less with greed than with a jungle appetite. Every now and again he emerged from a torpor of mastication to pour me some wine or ask me a question, then went back to his food again, crouched over the table, large elbows splayed on either side of his plate. We were cut off on three little islands; he and I, his stepmother, his father, and I felt the usual futile stirrings of discomfort. His father ate slowly, locked in a coma of his own, while the stepmother presided selflessly over the table, with her faint, tragic smile, moving, serving and offering plates with undemanding devotion.

Once, the old man said, "You see what that fool Mayor La Pira wants to do," and Franco responded, mouth full, with ready disgust, "What do you expect, then? He's a friar!" "They're all friars," his father said, and began with sudden gentleness to feed the cat with scraps from his plate. Their anti-clericalism was one of the links that bound them oddly but unmistakably together. It was a flat without crucifixes, without Sacred Hearts, and their tiny, votary electric bulbs. After the meal, Franco went with me, as usual, to the bus stop. "My dear!" he cried. "There is nothing in the world greater than football." "Well…" I said, and at once he laughed. "Right you are! I like to go with women – like a beast! But after that – football!" When the bus arrived he turned home at once, neither waving nor looking round as he walked back, purposeful and heavy shouldered.

A few days later, I came across Carlo in the town. It was in Via Tornabuoni, outside the ochre, compact elegance of the Palazzo Antinori. He was wearing a blue mackintosh, and when he half raised his arms in greeting he seemed for a moment like some great, shy bird, about to fly away. "*Oh! Buon giorno, dottore!*" I returned the greeting and felt a vague stirring of guilt at the memory of his dismay, on the football ground. "Have a coffee?"

I agreed without feeling much enthusiasm; between them, he and Franco had cast me for the role of prophet from afar, and on such an obstacle, conversation could only founder. His pleasure, besides, seemed excessive. "What luck, what luck!" he kept saying, as we went across the road, towards a bar. "I hoped to get a chance to talk to you, and now I have. I'm mad about English football: Franco's infected me!" At the zinc counter of the bar, he forcibly prevented my attempt to pay. "You must come round to my house! I told my parents I met you! I want to learn all I can about English football! One of these days, perhaps I'll go there." At this, he became almost ecstatic. "Ah, what an ambition! It's my greatest dream!"

As he talked, it seemed to me that he had not only acquired Franco's ideas, but some of his very physical mannerisms. A surface resemblance in their build, the colour of their hair, may partly have suggested this, yet the leonine voice – a surprise to me – was surely an echo of Franco. I asked him feebly whether he enjoyed his training, and he was off at once on another panegyric. "Of course! Franco's marvellous: magnificent! You don't know how intelligent he is: there's nothing about this game that he doesn't understand!" "And you'll join a professional club, I suppose?"

At this, exuberance seemed to drain away from him. His mouth drew tight, and he shook his head in dissatisfaction. "Who knows? Maybe yes, maybe no: it's a question of temperament. I think I'm talented, but there are too many things I understand in principle, and don't do right on the field." He talked on, with the ornate, astonishing fluency of the working-class Florentine. "With the help of the good Lord, I'll manage, and if I don't…" The life fled from his face again; for a moment, despair overwhelmed him. "I don't know what I'll do. I daren't even think about it. I don't know anything except football. I read a lot, but I haven't any culture; I'm ignorant... But excuse me, excuse me, I'm boring you." I told him he wasn't. "But how can you be interested in these things; a footballer in a junior team who isn't even a professional yet... perhaps never will be." "But Franco must believe in you," I said awkwardly.

Carlo shook his great head, and I noticed the powerful, footballer's neck. "Sometimes he doesn't treat me well. He knows I'm sensitive. The other day at the ground when he said those things to me, I didn't sleep all night. In front of you, too..." "You'll succeed," I said, "I'm sure you will," but the consolation seemed the emptier because he so plainly knew it for the evasion it was. "Let's hope so," he said, but he brightened when we parted outside the bar and he said, "I'll 'phone you up, soon: you must come to dinner."

For some reason, I never did, and it was not until July that I saw him or Franco again, after a winter spent in Rome. In the sun, the city had changed, so that it seemed unrelated to the brooding, ingoing, rejecting Florence of the colder months. Americans swarmed everywhere like a noisy, passive army: cropped haired, gloomy young men on mopeds, in shorts, lurid shirts, and three-quarter length socks; girls in sleeveless dresses, from Vassar and Radcliffe; legions of blue-haired middle-aged, spectacled matrons. Everywhere one was followed by the high, harsh clamour of the American female voice. It was as though the native Florentines had been driven from their squares and narrow streets, into the surrounding mountains. One morning, Franco telephoned to ask me to come with him to Viareggio. "I've got a car!" he shouted, this time in Italian. "I go like a madman, you'll see! I pass everybody on the road!"

It was hard to associate him with a car. For as long as I had known him, he had made his way about on a serviceable grey bicycle; how often had I waited in his flat, when he was late, for the ring of the bell and the tick-tick-tick of the slowly revolving wheel as he climbed the stairs, bicycle hoisted on his shoulder. I was sorry the bicycle had gone; it had somehow been a symbol of integrity, of his contempt for an over-monied sport in which the least of managers, the most banal of players, drove their *millecentos* and *seicentos*. This manager was a "blockhead"; that one "don't know nothing about football," but now, some of the sting seemed to be drawn from his contempt; buying the car was a step towards compromise.

Like the bicycle, it, too, was grey. It stood outside my *pensione* by the parapet of the Arno, sparkling in the early sunshine. "Fine car, eh?" Franco asked, briefly. Haste consumed him, making him seem more remote and distracted than ever. Upstairs, he had paced about my tiny room, refusing the offer of tea. "*Andiamo, andiamo!* If we don't go now, we'll be caught in the queue; we'll never get there till after midday!"

The day was going to be another superb one. It was only twenty past six, and the sun was still low in a bright, cloud-tufted sky, its mellow light dappling the tall, cool palaces, playing without response on the sluggish summer river. Our side of the Arno was still protected by shadow, in a brief morning armistice. Sitting in the back of the car was a tall, serious boy with wiry brown hair. In an aside, Franco told me, "My right-half: Bertuccini. Lovely player! I make a trial of him with Pisa."

He drove rapidly downriver, across the brute stone of the Ponte alla Carraia, through a city for the moment deserted and unspoiled, until at length we were on the white, anonymous stretch of road which would lead us to the coast.

I quickly understood his urgency. As we went on, Franco cutting ruthlessly past other cars, the traffic increased, till finally we were brought to a halt at the end of a line which wound out of sight, towards a toll gate. Franco swore quietly to himself and drummed his big hands on the steering wheel. Though the windows of the car were open and he was wearing the inevitable open necked white shirt, sweat was coursing down his red, flushed face in a network of tiny rivulets. "Bertuccini," he said, suddenly, without turning round. "How many cars have we passed?" "Twenty-three." "Keep the score, keep the score!"

The caravan moved slowly on until we reached the toll stage: with impatient generosity, Franco brushed away my offer of change. Then we were off again, faster than before, Franco hunched over the wheel, entering now into a private fantasy. He was Fangio, Musso or Stirling Moss, gloriously winning the Mille Miglia; mute, invisible thousands lined the road to cheer. "*Dio boia!*" he shouted in thicker and thicker Tuscan, "God the hangman! God the dog! Did you see how I went past that one, Bertuccini?" And Bertuccini, he, too, in the fantasy, kept the score; a calm co-driver. "Seventy... seventy-eight... Look out, there's that wardrobe behind us again." This for a large American car. And again, "Franco, there's a blonde driving that car, in front. Shall I whistle?" "Yes," said Franco, grimly between his teeth, "whistle," at which the serious Bertuccini leaned gravely out of the window and let forth a sudden, terrifying blast of sound.

Once, we stopped for petrol. A tanned, attractive girl had got out of a car which already stood at the pump, and Franco prowled round her in a wide semi-circle, his lips pursed in a long, soundless whistle. Past the cypresses we went, running the hideous gauntlet of coloured wooden advertisements which lined the road on either side – for coffee, petrol, motor tyres. Far off, to our right, one could just see the Apuan Alps swelling through cloud, huge, majestic and contemptuous.

"How many cars, Bertuccini?" "A hundred and three." "And to think," he said, turning to me in proud delight, "that I've only been driving two months! If I'd started at sixteen, I'd have been another Musso!" He edged out of the line of cars for another foray, but the advent of a massive truck on the other side of the road forced him to withdraw. Then he was out again, circling precariously round a Lancia, edging his way into a traffic gap, crying in half apology, "Because there's no discipline in Italy. . . ."

At last we were on the outskirts of the vulgar little town, among the cool pinewoods, one of a line of cars that had slowed and faltered, now that the goal was in sight.

"Bertuccini!" Franco said. "What a woman I had last night. *Che donnuccia!* Six times, I promise you, six times!" "*Bella roba,*" Bertuccini dutifully said, but already Franco had left the subject, like a discarded toy, and was talking to me. "I have five of my boys here." "Including Carlo ?" "Yes," he replied, indifferently, "he's here." "Is he doing well?" "A blockhead! He will never become a good footballer!" "Then why do you keep him?" A heave of the shoulders. *"Chi lo so?"*

From behind us, Bertuccini said, "He's a good ball player." Franco agreed with a grimace of indifference. "And your centre-half?" I asked. "*Ottimo, ottimo*; always improving."

Slowly we made our way into the little town, bright and noisy and jerry-built, a summer colony of Florence. Each narrow street was indistinguishable from the next with its pale stone houses, its chromium bars, its *rosticcurie*, its extinct neon signs, its shuffling morning hordes in sandals, shorts and raffia hats. Across the streets, bright banners advertised the February carnival, but one could not visualise this town in winter. It had too strong an air of transience, a town run up by property-men for a season which would be dismantled and carried away with terrible, ruthless speed as soon as that season was over.

Franco stopped the car in front of one of the featureless houses and got out, leaving me with Bertuccini. To break the silence, I turned to him and asked, "Will Carlo 'make it,' do you think ?" "He may do," the boy replied. "*E un ragazzo serio*: he lives for football. But he doesn't get on with Franco; who knows why?" Who, indeed? "He reads a lot," Bertuccini said, gratuitously.

"He's always reading."

At that moment, Franco reappeared, at the head of his boys, great voice thundering like a friendly sergeant major's. Carlo was there, greeting me with simple delight, so that again I felt guilty of a masquerade. The centre-half was there, too, a smiling Hermes, quite without problems, and there were several other boys whom I vaguely remembered from the football stadium. All of them wore shorts, all of them, even Carlo, were tanned and relaxed.

They bundled into the car and we drove on to the sea front, past the swollen abortions of the big hotels. The beach was a benign concentration camp, each section carefully partitioned from the next, each entered by a coloured wooden arch on which one read its name – "Italia," "Two Sisters," "Victory," "Miramare." Our beach was called "La Bella Speranza."

Franco swaggered through the arch as though it had been erected for his triumph, to be met at once by a fusillade of greeting, *Ciao Franco! Oh, Franco!* greeted by boys, by men, by toothless women bathing attendants, he himself smiling a smile so cheerful as for once to be almost self-conscious, shortly returning a salutation here, another there. It was at this beach that his young players spent the summer each year, financed by himself, while he scoured the country in search of *ingaggi*; contracts with professional clubs for the following season.

We changed in turn in a small, dark communal dressing room. When I came out, Franco was waiting for me at the end of the boardwalk, a huge, bronzed figure in his blue bathing slip, which seemed no more than a formal dash of colour at his loins. We moved out on to the hot, pale sand, moved between the beach umbrellas, the serried battalions of deck chairs that turned the beach into a congested, three sided square. Everywhere one looked there was noise and intimacy; people sat shoulder to shoulder – except for the grandmothers, wizened in their ugly black – gathered on the shore in talkative knots, moved up and down in phalanx.

Franco had scarcely gone five yards when he was stopped by a man almost as large as himself, whose camera, slung around his bare chest, showed him to be a beach photographer. The man greeted him with a robust mixture of banter and welcome. "What about these footballers of yours? They do nothing all day but go with women!"

"Not true, not true!" Franco roared, looking out to sea. "I've told all of them: no more than three times a week!" And he resumed his march, only to be stopped again by the blue jerseyed *bagnino* and again, seconds later, by a bald young man in bathing trunks.

And so it continued, Franco moving slowly, powerfully up and down the beach with his rolling, swaggering walk, a little posse of young footballers and boys at his shoulders, greeted by all with the amusement tinged with admiration which one might reserve for some faintly comic institution.

After a while, four of us took a blue bathing float and rowed out for a swim. The water was a pale, domesticated green. On it, a motor-boat with a loud hailer coursed tirelessly up and down, blaring its intrusions at the beaches; exhortations to go to this dancing place, to drink that orangeade. Franco swam well, as one expected, moving through the water with the speed and power of a destroyer: around him, his players gambolled like acolytes about a sea god.

It was past two o'clock before we were back at the *pensione* for lunch, served al fresco on the cool, trellised *terrazza*. Franco sat shirtless at the head of the table, keeping up a roaring, straight faced monologue, fluent, ruthless, cynical and at times immensely comic. The boys looked on, beaming and nudging one another with delight, smiling at me from time to time as though to ask, "What do you think of him, eh?"

"Meneghini!" thundered Franco. "What a manager! That no good! *Quel cialtrone!* So he's going to Brazil to study training. And what's he going to find out when he gets there? That at Rio they've got a beach seven miles long, where everybody plays: women, children, old men, cripples!" He took an enormous forkful of spaghetti, and resumed. When the explosion came it was from the blue, curiously under-determined. The meal was nearly over, we were eating fruit, and Franco was pillorying yet another manager. *"Un' testa di cazzo!* A half-wit! With an idiot's face – like yours!" he added, gesturing vaguely towards Carlo.

Carlo rose at once to his feet, his face contorted, and cried in a high, anguished voice. "Franco: *ma to sei sadico!* You're a sadist! Why must you always persecute me? It's not fair! I know my own defects perfectly well: I try and do something about them – saying things like that all the time doesn't help me! Well, I can't put up with it any more. Maybe I am ugly. Maybe I never will succeed as a footballer. But you: what's going to happen to you? It's a weakness in you, that you have to keep treating me like this. You'll ruin yourself, Franco, I swear it; you'll ruin yourself!"

He stopped for a moment, amidst dead silence. Franco was gaping at him in sheer astonishment, a banana half way to his mouth; as though he had gently prodded a dog which responded by leaping at his throat. The *signora* had come to the open door and was looking on with anxious astonishment. Carlo was crying in earnest, now; tears ran steadily down the tanned cheeks of his gentle, ugly face. He tried to speak again, gulped and stammered, then at last managed to shout, quick and hoarse, "You shouldn't treat me like that!

82

It's not human!" Then he turned clumsily away from the table, upsetting his chair, and pushed his way blindly past the *signora*, into the house.

Silence continued for a full minute after his departure, then Franco said, in a grumbling voice without conviction, "*Ma quel cretino.*"

Two days later, in Florence, Carlo telephoned me. His voice was hesitant and stuttering. "*Dottore*, if you wouldn't mind... I'd like to see you: it's important for me." I agreed to meet him that afternoon, in the Piazza della Repubblica.

In these hot tourist months, the vulgar irrelevance of the piazza no longer gave offence. One did not grudge it to the invading armies; it was theirs as much as the city's, more than the city's, with its four brassy cafes, its air cooled multiple store and its coloured advertisements.

I was five minutes late, and Carlo was waiting for me, as I knew he would be, sitting, white shirted, under a red umbrella, his crisp sleeves buttoned to the wrists. The cafe he had chosen was on the Oltrarno, less popular side, gaudily placarded with English tourist menus, painted on shiny white boards. He rose to his feet, arms moving in the familiar, arrested gesture. "*Dottore dottore* I'm sorry... what will you have? A cognac?"

I said I would have a coffee, and made him sit down; his body trembled with agitation. He waited in anguished silence till the waiter came to take our order, then, when the man was barely three paces away, he blurted out, "I wanted to apologise!"

"But why? There's no reason..."

His mouth contracted, he looked down at the table and he said, "I shouldn't have behaved like that. I'm ashamed. It was a great embarrassment for you."

"It wasn't..." I said, ineptly, wishing he'd stop.

"I wanted to explain. There's no excuse: it was unforgivable; but if you knew the things that had been happening, perhaps you wouldn't judge me too harshly."

I said I was in no position to judge him at all, but he scarcely seemed to hear. "I don't admire Franco any more," he said. "You understand – not as a man. As a coach, yes, he's great; great," and his eyes lit up, as though despite himself. "But I've thought a lot since I saw you, in the winter. I've read a lot, too; I've begun to understand things. And I've realised for one thing that I'm never going to be a great footballer, Franco's right about that... no, no, he's right: not because I'm ugly, that's got nothing to do with it; but because I'm not gifted enough: now I know it. And knowing it's made me less dependent on him. I became objective, you understand; I saw things I didn't see before. As a human being... well, now I don't esteem him."

At the table behind us, a loud voice was saying, "So I told him, do you know I can get these things for half the price back home?" "Since he got the car," Carlo said, in agitation, "I've told him, 'Franco, you'll destroy yourself. Always with women... stick to football, or it'll be the end of you.' He used to spend hours with us, just talking football, but now it's different. He didn't used to care much about money, but now he talks about it all the time."

He leaned across the table earnestly and said, "Perhaps you don't believe me. He shows another side to you... But it's all true, I swear it."

"Then I'm sorry," I said.

"I tell him," Carlo cried, "very well, I'm a failure, I admit it! *Un calciatore fallito!* But with you, Franco, where's it going to end?"

It was more than a year before I visited Florence again. Franco, when I telephoned him, greeted me with his usual roar of welcome. "OOH! My dear! You come my house for dinner!"

I came. Nothing had visibly changed, save the arrival of a television set. It stood in the far left-hand corner of the dining room, a cynosure, monopolising attention, strangling conversation. Franco watched it from his place at table, chewing slowly, half-hypnotised. If I spoke to him, he laid a hand on my arm, as though to reassure me of his sympathy, despite his evident distraction. After a while, I asked him what had happened to Carlo.

He shrugged, without taking his eyes from the screen. "That cretin! He doesn't play any more."

"Not at all?"

"He's got a job at a school." He laughed. "You know what he's doing? Teaching gymnastics to boys of six and seven."

"So he gave up football," I said.

"*Ma!* With a face like that."

I telephoned Carlo, and we met the following day, at the same cafe as before. Once more, he had preceded me, once more, he greeted me with embarrassing enthusiasm. And yet I could sense at once that a change had taken place, as though the very admission of failure, the abandoning of ambition, had given him a sudden independence.

"Franco told me you'd given up football," I said. "I wanted to tell you I was sorry."

"It's very kind of you, very kind." He shook his head, slowly and miserably. "It wasn't easy. You can't give up your greatest love easily. I keep away from football now: if I go to watch Fiorentina, or to Rifredi, it makes me want to cry. I've got a little job now at a school, teaching physical education. It isn't much, but it's a beginning. I'm working for my certificate."

In disillusion, he seemed to have gained not only maturity but authority; perhaps it came from his new job. Afterwards, we walked together through the darkening streets; beside a newspaper kiosk in the nearby portico, Franco was arguing loudly with a group of football fans.

When Carlo saw him, he shied, almost imperceptibly, like a horse recovered from a recent fall; then he went on again and said, his face uncertain, "*Ciao, Franco.*"

"*Ciao*, gymnast." Franco said, and greeted me more cordially. "One of my ex-pupils," he addressed the group. "He couldn't play football so now he's trying to teach gymnastics to babies."

Carlo's face was tense, unsmiling, appallingly vulnerable. He did not reply, but he stared at Franco, now, with neither wonder nor admiration." "What are you showing them, eh?" Franco asked, "how to get off with women – like you do?"

Carlo's face quivered, and for a moment I thought it was going to disintegrate, as it had at Viareggio. Then he said, "Caro Franco, you never change. You never change at all."

I left him at the corner of Via Strozzi; he did not speak again till then. Then he said, "I've failed as a footballer. I've failed."

"But Carlo, you've got your new job."

"I've failed once," he insisted, "in the thing I most wanted to do, most wanted to be. Who knows if I can ever succeed in anything else?"

"I'm sure you will," I said, as we shook hands.

He smiled then, a pale, sad smile and said. "You're too kind to me; but you don't know my deficiencies."

I watched him as he walked away, broad shoulders stooped in his blue mackintosh, moving joylessly among the passers-by. But I did not feel sorry for Carlo.

My brother and me

We looked at each other through the grille, my brother and me. He didn't say nothing, I didn't say nothing, there was no need. This look; we'd give it each other before. One day at Borough Stadium. I'd run for a ball, hadn't got it, overshot the goal line, fallen over some berk of a photographer, stood up, facing the crowd – and looked straight into his eyes. Him there on the terraces. He didn't smile, neither of us did. Just this look, like: I could be you and you could be me, which was true. Me on the terraces, him on the field. Me in the nick, him visiting me. So what was there to say?

My mother crying, the old man embarrassed, twisting his scarf in his hands like he did when that was how he felt; big hands, the kind you get when you've used them all your life to work in factories. I'd look at them and say to myself, not me, I'd rather work with my feet than my hands. As for Tom, my brother, he seemed cheerful, the only one of us that smiled.

"All right, Tom?" my father said, and he said, "Yeah, all right, not too bad considering." Which meant considering he was up for murder and could go down for twenty-five years.

"Food all right?" my father asked, which was a silly question, but what *did* you say?

"Could be worse," Tom said, which was Tom. Never took nothing too serious, which was good and bad. I mean now it was good, but other times it was bad, which was why he was here, really, here in the Scrubs.

There'd been a time when he'd looked the better player, a long time in fact, almost right the way through school. International trial, where I never got one. London schoolboys. I don't mind admitting, though I didn't like it then, if it came to ability, he had more. Marvellous on the ball. Balance, body swerve, two good feet – I'm still much stronger on my right. But never bothered, it was all a giggle. Trials with the Hammers, trials with Fulham, trials with Arsenal. Stayed there a while, then turned it in though they all wanted him, in the beginning.

"Nice and handy for the Rangers here," he said. "You can hear the crowd, and all. Next time you're playing at Loftus Road, come in and see me, Bob."

"Okay," I said, "you're on."

"Mind," he said, "Pentonville would have been better, wouldn't it? Nearer. Holloway better still. I wouldn't have minded getting in among all them birds."

The old man nodded across at Mum, who was still crying, meaning give it up, then he said, "We've talked to your solicitor. He seemed... Well, it don't look hopeless."

"Oh, him," said Tom. "Yeah, I known worse." In fact, him and me, we'd known quite a few – juvenile court, magistrates' court. Never anything too serious before, bar the once, mostly aggro and, in my case, nothing since I was sixteen, which was a punch-up in a pub over King's Cross with a lot of loud-mouthed Jocks down for the England-Scotland. Tom was in it, too. When the club found out about it, Borough, they had me in the office and the Manager said this was the first and last time, any more of it, and they'd cancel my apprenticeship. Which was really why we went our separate ways, the time when it come home to me that I could go one way or the other, Tom's way or Borough's way, because with Tom, even though he was younger than me, a year younger, it was obvious which way he'd go – the way he was going now.

And I decided, I'd be a player, which seems easy now, but wasn't easy then. Giving up boozing, giving up aggro, giving up your mates, with Tom round you all the time to show you what you're missing. "Come on!" he'd say. "Let's go up Euston, sort out some of them United fans!" or "Coming up the Mercer's Arms tonight? Lot of the lads'll be there, plenty of birds, as well." And I'd want to go, I won't pretend I didn't, but I'd say no, no thanks, Tom, not this time. And he'd look at me, he'd smile, the corners of his mouth would turn up, he'd say, "Sorry, Bob. Forgot you had to be in bed by ten, old son."

But I'd seen the way they lived, our first-team players there at Borough, driving down the ground in Jags and Mercs, hand-made shirts, ninety-quid suits. I wanted that. It was worth giving up bit for that. You think it was easy? And with him?

Sometimes I wished I'd never joined a London club, sometimes I wished I'd pissed off somewhere in the provinces, Sheffield, Leeds, Birmingham, any poxy old place, just to get away, to live in digs with other young apprentices like most of them at Borough did, where you didn't have what you was giving up thrown at you every day. Seeing him putting on the gear, the old bovver boots and braces in the skinhead days, later on the flared jeans and the crombie, when for me it was going to be watch the telly and bed by eleven. Hearing when he'd pulled a bird.

"You're doing the right thing, Bob," my father used to say. "I'm proud of you. I'll be honest, I never thought you'd have the discipline," and what I'd think was, fuck the discipline, there was too much bloody discipline, discipline all day, more discipline at night. Those days, those nights, I'd find myself thinking maybe he was right, Tom, maybe he knew something. Because they didn't, not the blokes that were meant to, or not many of them.

You turned apprentice, you went to a club thinking there'd be people you'd respect, people who'd teach you things, and what you found were twats, little men that tried to bully you, that tried to stop you playing, that never, never let you enjoy yourself. What we'd always liked, Tom and me, was taking people on, beating them, committing them, nutmegging them. We were ball players, we liked to do things with the ball. We was always having competitions, who could juggle it the longest, first with tennis balls, later on with full-sized footballs. He was better, but I was good as well.

But at Borough, they didn't want none of that. "Square it, give it, get rid of it!" Great on one-twos, they were. "Don't try and beat the man, let the ball do the work! Give it and go! Move for the quick return!" Robots was what they wanted, not footballers, and it all came down from the top, as I'd find out when I got into the first team; from that fat-arsed little sod who was the manager and who, to me, knew nothing about football. "Give it, give it!" If you took someone on, you might lose the ball, and what a terrible thing that would be. "But you might get past them!" I'd say, when I'd been there a little while, when I'd got the confidence. "Go by one bloke, and you commit someone else."

"Lose it," they'd say, "and they commit someone else."

This was the first big row I had there – the second, if you count the punch-up. It was a youth team game and Ronnie Noakes, the youth coach, who was a right idiot, was bollocking me: "Give it, move it, why don't you move it?" Till at half-time I called him a cunt, and he pulled me off.

Into the Manager again, Ted Wrigley, little fat arse. "I understand you used obscene language to one of our coaches."

"I was provoked, wasn't I?" I said.

"You were not provoked. I've heard exactly what happened. You persistently refused to do what you were told."

"I didn't agree with it," I said.

"In other words, you think you know better than our youth team coach."

"He won't let me play," I said.

"What do you think would happen if everybody in a team just played for themselves?" he asked me. He was clever like that. He could twist things. It was only afterwards you thought, I don't play for myself, I play my own way, that's all, but I was still very young and he'd got everything going for him, the big desk, the big office, me being only an apprentice he could just kick out. Later on, I didn't forget it.

So what it came down to was, either I apologised, or I was out. And I apologised. It choked me. I hated myself. What I wanted to do was hit the little bastard, Ronnie Noakes, little blond, square-headed bloke that treated you like he had you in the Army. I held my hand out, I let him shake it, but he never knew how near it came to landing on his bloody chin. And doing it, I thought of Tom, what he'd have said, how he'd have laughed at me, taken the mickey. I didn't tell him, never said a word at home about it, knowing that would only make it worse. It was bad enough as it was.

Every Saturday when I came in and we'd been playing at home, he'd be on about the aggro, how they'd done up these Liverpool supporters at Euston, how they'd sorted out the United fans on the terraces when they tried to take the Cresty Road End. Often he'd have a big bruise on his face or a cut, but it never bothered him. Mum was the one it bothered, she'd fussed over him ever since he was little with a load of blond curls and, as for the old man, I reckon in a funny way he was proud of Tom; Tom couldn't do no wrong.

Now and again it would come out. Him and I might be sitting in the kitchen, having a cup of tea, or in front of telly, and he'd say, "Tell you the truth, Bob, I never expected you to do so well. If I'd had to put money on one or the other of you as schoolboys, it would have been Tom. It just shows you, but you done marvellous," meaning it was Tom he'd wanted to do well. I wasn't too thick to see that.

Me and Tom, on the terraces, we'd been a right old pair. Fists, boots, nut. When we really got going we'd use anything, except weapons, we never went in for them, which was why I couldn't believe it when I heard what had happened to him. It just wasn't Tom.

"He's changed, Bob," the old man said. "You haven't noticed the change in him. As you've done better, he's got wilder," and when I thought about it, I supposed it was true.

Now and again he'd come to our games, him and his mates, them early days, though at first it was a bit of a giggle for them; youth matches, South

East Counties and that, just a few dozens on the terraces. Even when I got in the Reserve side it was usually dead, especially when we was playing at Borough Stadium, all them miles and miles of empty concrete steps. I'd hear his voice: "Go on, Bobby, set 'em alight, son!", taking the piss. Afterwards he'd sometimes tell me, "Honest, Bob, you were rubbish today," which was normal enough, the way we'd always gone at each other, though now and then there seemed to be a bit of needle in it.

We'd always been Borough supporters, Tom and me. It was our local club, you could walk there from our home, and every Saturday that was where we'd go – us and our mates on the Cresty Road terraces behind the goal, which was our territory.

When I got in the first team, I was seventeen, which meant Tom was sixteen. He'd left school at fifteen like I had, and he must have had half a dozen jobs already: messenger, delivery boy, window cleaning, work in a garage. "Poxy jobs," he'd say. "I wish I was a layabout like Bob here. Ponce around in the fresh air a couple of hours a day, then home for lunch."

"Bob's worked hard," the old man would tell him.

"Work?" he'd say. "Call that work?"

"You'd know if you tried it," I'd say, because to me it certainly wasn't play.

A lot of times I felt like packing it in. There was only two things kept me going. One was my pride, and the other, like I said, was what I knew I could get if I ever made it, the cars and the money and the birds. I didn't notice the real big stars making no sacrifices, switching their lights out at ten o'clock. They'd be up the Sportsman or down the Astor, knocking back the Bacardi and rum and chatting up the crumpet. Or maybe at one of these charity dinners – there was a lot of them – frilled shirts and velvet dinner jackets swigging away till well after midnight. That'd do me.

The other thing was to prove to all those bastards I was right, all those people I despised, that my way was the right way – which was what effect they had. First of all it sickened you, realising they was all twats, that there was no one really understood the game, thinking, so why go on? Then with a little more success you thought, I'll show 'em. I knew I'd got it, I knew I could do it though, at the same time, I knew it was a gamble, even without all the people who were getting in your way. You could break a leg, do your knee ligaments, and that was that; nothing left, the whole thing finished, while you was still in your twenties. There'd been two or three that happened to while I'd been at Borough.

My first League game was a tremendous game, though. Against Newcastle, and it was at home, so I knew that when we ran on to the field, and probably while we were kicking in, they'd be there behind the Cresty Road goal shouting for me, Tom and the lads.

And we did kick into that goal, and I could hear them though I couldn't see them: "Make a name, Bob! Take 'em apart, Bobby!" Best of all, I scored in that game. Half-way through the second half, a long throw in from the right, on the trolley, *whoosh!*, you know the feeling when you catch it properly, just like hitting a golf ball. I could tell right away there was nothing going to stop it, and you should have heard the roar. I didn't so much hear it, in fact, as feel it, in my stomach, rising up all warm in me just like a wave. I stood there with my arms held up, and they all came rushing in to hug me. It made up for a lot, that moment.

It must have been my fourth or fifth home game that I nutted somebody, and it was the Cresty Road End, again, in front of that goal. We were playing Leeds and one of their blokes slid me from behind, right into my Achilles tendon. I didn't even think, I just got up and nutted him, and down he went. Luckily the play had moved on up the other end and the referee had his back turned, the linesman didn't really see it, or said he didn't, and I got away with it. I was only booked, not sent off.

Monday, into the manager again, little fat arse. "You've got to make up your mind."

"Make up my mind about what?"

"Either you're a professional footballer and you accept the responsibilities, or you can go back to being a hooligan." What I wanted to do then was smash up his office and him with it: all the poncey photographs, all the little gadgets on the desk, all the bloody pennants on the walls. "Fuck you," I wanted to tell him. "Put me on the transfer list." But I bottled it, I didn't say nothing, I sat there with my head down. All I answered was, "He came right through me."

"I know he did," he said. "I know you were provoked. That's part of the game, people provoking you, and if you're going to react like you do, then nine times out of ten you'll be off the field. What use are you to us if we have to play with ten men every other game?" Which was fair, yet it wasn't fair. Whatever he said I'd no respect for, because I didn't respect the man.

That was nice, that: hooligan. I suppose you could call Tom a hooligan, doing what he wanted, doing it his own way, putting two fingers up at everybody. Which was the next time I got into trouble – putting two fingers up. At Manchester City, in November. The crowd had been getting at me all the game, "Chester is a wanker!"

Two minutes from the end, it was still nil-nil, I scored: caught the ball with my thigh, saw the keeper off his line, flicked it over his head. Then I looked up at the terraces above the goal and I give them the old two fingers. Unfortunately we were Match of the Day that night on television. This time, though, he didn't send for me, he couldn't really. I'd won the match, hadn't I? I got them the points.

Tom was chuffed, like you'd expect. "That showed them northern tosses," he said. There was a bit of talk of me being had up by the Football Association for bringing the game into disrepute and all that crap, but nothing ever came of it. It made me laugh when I thought of what Tom could get away with Saturday after Saturday on them terraces: punch-ups, putting the boot in. I stick two fingers up, don't hurt nobody, and it's like I've got the whole country on my back.

It was about then that Tom went inside for the first time. As I said, he'd been in trouble often enough before and so had I, but he had been fined twenty quid, maybe fined fifty quid, or now and again a detention centre for a few Saturday afternoons, cleaning floors and that. This time, though, he got nicked for doing a shop.

It was stupid really, he admitted it himself. A few of them got pissed, it was more of a lark than anything. Three months was what he got – in Wandsworth. The old man was choked, my mother cried a lot. I was sorry that it happened, but beyond that it didn't affect me that much, like it didn't seem to affect him. That was the risk he took, wasn't it? Like if you play football, you can always break a leg.

I was still in and out of bother. Most of what happened to me happened in home games, and most of that was at the Cresty Road End. I never noticed it till a local paper bloke from round Manor House, Ron Smithson, one of the few reporters that I'd even talk to, said to me one day, "You know where you do it all, Bob? The things that get you into trouble? It's always down there, right in front of that Cresty Road goal."

"Do I?" I said. "I never thought about it," but now I did. I realised maybe he was right.

"It's spoiling you, Bob," he said, "with your ability," which I'd take from him, though not from the little fat arse.

"Forget 'em," he said, "them terraces. They're nothing to do with you no more."

Funnily enough, while Tom was inside, from January to April, I didn't have no trouble. It never occurred to me at the time, and it may just have been that no one got at me, which was how it always started – though I'll admit I liked it when it *did* happen and Tom told me, "Done him properly, Bob, the dirty sod. All the lads was pleased."

I was eighteen then and was on a hundred quid a week, plus bonuses. I was driving a Lotus, I bought any gear I fancied; and I was still living at home because that was the club rule. If you was single, either you lived in digs or you lived at home. It was awkward, because Tom was still there, too, and although he didn't do too bad – window cleaning, car spraying, labouring and that – there wasn't no comparison. Now and again I'd lend him the car, though I stopped that after he got pissed and smashed it up. Sometimes he'd borrow money off me which I knew I'd never see again, but it still couldn't bring us into line.

He could get stroppy now, which he never used to be. "Here he is, the star! How's the boy wonder today then?" Once I thumped him, when I'd had a bad game and we'd lost. The old man had to break it up. That was something Tom could never understand, the pressures. All he could see was my picture in the papers, the gear I wore, the birds I pulled. He didn't know what it was like, sitting in that dressing room before a match, your guts like water, fifty thousand out there waiting to crucify you if you put a foot wrong; what it was to take orders from berks that didn't know nothing; to get stick from ignorant Press men. I told Tom once, "I earn every fucking penny."

And I was going to enjoy it while I had it. All this crap about saving that I heard at the club and from Mum at home. Quite a few of the players was savers, the young ones got the club to invest half their money for them, lived like they was still poor, and in fifteen years they might have enough to open up a newsagent – if they didn't want to become managers, which ninety-nine per cent did. As far as I was concerned, they could stuff it. I could really see myself crawling to a lot of poxy directors, telling me how to pick the team.

The game it all happened was a Cup tie, home to Wolves, Sixth Round, one of the best I'd ever played in. It was me that won it too. They went one up in the first few minutes when our keeper dropped a cross, we equalised then, with about ten minutes left, I got the ball twenty yards or so inside their half, and I started moving towards their goal, the Cresty Road End goal. It was a muddy day – if you committed a defender he'd got no chance to recover. I went past one. I heard Frank, our centre-foward, calling for it on my left; dummied like I was going to pass to him, went the other way, between two more of them, and hit it with my right foot, bang, just from the edge of the box. It was a lovely shot, the keeper never got near it, and it went in to his right, high and diagonally, rising all the way, smack in the top corner. Magic! I gave the old punch in the air salute to the crowd behind the goal and they was going spare, in fact I could see there was a bit of aggro about as well. That was when it happened, though, of course, I thought nothing of it then.

I was sitting in the dressing room afterwards, just out of the bath, feeling well pleased, when Rod, our physio, come in with a funny expression on his face and said, "There's a copper outside wants to see you, Bob."

"Me?" I said. "What have I done?" It was habit, I suppose – right away I tried to think what it could be.

Naturally the lads thought it was a great laugh. "Maybe he's a Wolves fan!" one of them said, and another one shouted, "I'll give you an alibi, Bobby!"

"Can't it wait?" I asked, but Rod said no, the bloke said it couldn't wait, and I went out like I was, in a towel. In the corridor was this big copper in a peak cap, silver pips on his shoulder, a superintendent or something. Could I come down to the station? There was someone there who said he was my brother.

I got really worried then. I asked, "Is he hurt or something?"

"He's not hurt," he said.

"You mean he done somebody?" I asked him, and he told me, "He's been charged."

"Is he a bloke about my height?" I asked. "Blue eyes and curly hair?"

"That's him," he said, so that's how I knew.

I went down to the nick with him right away, and when I got there, Tom seemed a bit dazed. There was a big bruise on his forehead, when I got quite near him I could smell the beer on his breath. He kept saying, "I don't know what happened. I don't know what happened," which he still says. He still don't know why he hit the bloke, though now he says the fellow come at him, it was in self-defence.

It don't look too good, though his lawyer says they'll maybe bring it down to manslaughter. What'd he get, then? Ten years, fifteen years? How long'll I stay in this game, ten years, fifteen years? I reckon we could be finishing together.

Hanger-on

He was a creature of railway hotels, car parks, dining-cars, bleak corridors which led past dressing-rooms. Here, where no one was at home, he too seemed to have his place. His face was somehow in context, long and pink and guileless, gold spectacled, the blond hair swept carefully back in a pale, Brylcreemed wave, the large white teeth bared in his well wishing smile.

Appropriately, it was in a railway hotel that I first met him; a hotel with grey, smoke grimed walls, inhabited at weekends by football teams coming from the North to play in London; an oasis of the game. Outside it, on a Saturday morning, would stand small, scruffy knots of boys with autograph albums and scrapbooks, pouncing with avid speed on players who emerged.

"Come on, that's 'im! Sign; please sir; sign!" And they would surround the player in a gesturing, chattering, determined group, a forest of hands waving like tendrils in his face, extending books and pens and pencils.

Inside, the hotel was cramped and stiflingly heated, a confusing series of disused rooms, full of chairs and baize tables, as though awaiting some phantom convention. The smell of breakfasts floated out of the dining-room, and in the corridors one came across plump, bald, bustling men, with gold watch chains and hearty provincial accents – the club directors.

I was talking to some players in the bar when he came in. He entered with brisk assurance, certain of his welcome, striding across to our group at once, talking in quick monotone, covering us all with a soft lather of words. The cadence of the voice, the short "a's", showed that he had once had a Northern accent, but it had almost disappeared now, worn down and honed away. The voice had lost its edge, and the words rolled on, steadily and fluently, like a stream of oil. "Joe," he said, urgently, squatting down, like a supplicant, beside a player's chair. "Did you get my note? You knew I was coming, didn't you? I saw Charlie last week, and he said if he ran into George he'd tell him to let you know I was in London now." I tried to place each Christian name in turn, and when he was introduced to me he said at once, "Hello, Brian. We haven't met before, but I was talking to Jack Tomlin about you the other day, and he asked me if I knew you."

Tomlin was a famous manager: it was a good ploy.

His name, he told me, was Peter Bridge, and the footballers seemed to accept him readily enough. He went on talking to them intimately, seriously persuasively, as though they were all involved in some embracing family concern. I wondered who he could be, for his name meant nothing to me: an ex-player, perhaps, an old school friend of one of the team. I was surprised when he asked, suddenly and anxiously, "Joe, you've got a ticket for me?"

The player, a small, boyish Scotsman, grinned and reassured him, "Ay, you'll be all right, Peter." "And will I be able to come in the team coach? Have you asked Tom?" Tom was the club manager.

"I'll see what I can do, Peter, but he's not keen, is he, lads?"

At this, a startled look of pain came over Peter's raw, pink face and he said, "But he's always let me; I've always done it before."

As I got up, to report a different match, he called at me, with the same expression of concern, "You're not coming to Highbury? We'll get together... I'm in London... we'll have a cup of tea. Hey, give me your number."

I said, without warmth, that he could get it from my newspaper, and left. The following Monday, he rang me.

"This is Peter, Peter Bridge. How are you keeping?"

At first I did not recognise his monotone. "You *know*," he said, his voice pained. "On Saturday, in the hotel. With Joe and the United players."

I told him then, guilty and over-cordial, that I remembered him, and he was mollified at once, talking on without inhibition, one old friend to another.

"Well, it's nice to have met you," he said at last. "When are we going to have that cup of tea? Tell me where you live. If I'm passing that way one afternoon, I could drop in."

I said I was not often in during the afternoons.

"Oh, I see. Busy man, eh?" There was no edge to the words. "Well, look, I'll ring you again next week; during my lunch hour. That's the only chance I get during the day. Goodbye for now." And he had rung off, leaving me to wonder what his job could be.

I saw him again the following Saturday, standing outside the official entrance at Tottenham, among the fat, sanguine men with handfuls of black market tickets. He wore, surprisingly, a camel hair coat, which looked expensive and new but did not suit him: a pathetic attempt to seem "wide", a man about the West End, which only rendered him the more provincial. He was wearing his anxious look again.

"I'm waiting for Johnny Jackson," he said. "I wrote and told him I'd be here. I know he's down with the lads, because the papers said this morning there was still a chance he might be playing. If you see him, tell him I'm here, will you? He'll have a ticket for me."

I went into the great, grey desert of a car park, where journalists and directors and directors' friends stood about talking to one another, but the players had all gone in to change. He would have to go on the terraces, then, I thought, without much sympathy. For I had assessed him now; he was a fringe man, a cadger, a pale, harmless parasite who lurked on the edges of the game, relying on other people's tolerance and indulgence.

When I turned round he was there at my elbow, smiling now, a ticket in his hand, saying happily, "Well, after all that! Hey, just a minute, there's Arthur – I'll be back!" and he was off across the car park to greet a reporter.

He was no ordinary fringe man.

In the weeks that followed, he turned up so often that I wondered how it was that we had never met before. He was everywhere; in hotels, in trains, outside stadiums, talking earnestly to managers, players, journalists; man to man, a fellow expert, life-long acquaintance. His telephone calls to me continued, each drawn out, unless I was careful, to lengths of screaming triviality, each full of gossip, Christian names, intrusive proposals to meet.

I gave in at last, and we met after an evening football match. We sat in a dingy cafe with marble-topped, tea splashed tables, menu chalked up on a blackboard, a juke box pounding rock 'n' roll in a corner, teenage boys and girls with weird attire and hair styles sitting apart in rigidly celibate groups. It was here that I at last found out what he did, but only by a direct question. "I'm in a bank," he said, all in one breath. His mouth twitched, and he looked quickly away as though he were afraid to be overheard. "Down in Finsbury Park, but I don't want to stay there; I just took it so I could get to London; jumped at it. What I'm after is a job in your game."

"What, journalism?"

"Yes, sports page." The subject had been turned; he was easier now. "I'm keeping my fingers crossed at the moment. Reg Williams said he'd see if he could get me a job on the *Mail*."

"But," I said, incredulously, "you've got to have a Union card..."

"Just part time," he answered, airily. "Anyway, to begin with. I give him bits of sports gossip and stuff every now and then. And Bob Robinson says he might be able to fix me up doing match reports for the *Sunday Pictorial*.

Then, if everything came off, I could go on to the staff of one of them, after a while."

I wished him luck, and wondered whether to believe him. If journalism were really his ambition, why wasn't he following the well worn track from local paper to provincial "evening" to Fleet Street, like the rest?

"I've done a lot of articles," he said. "I'd like you to read them. Reg Williams read them, and Bob Robinson's got them now. When he's finished with them, I'll bring them over."

I was going to protest, but the moment passed. He looked across the room at a girl with a heavily rouged face, puffed cheeks and a dark ponytail and said, "One of those would suit me. What sort of love life have you got? You're a dark one, eh?" Then he was talking about football again, as if the subject had never been changed.

"What do you think of Alan Coxhead? Out of the game for life, and only 24. It really upset me, you know, it really did, because I've known him for years. In fact we were practically brought up together; like brothers." He looked sadly out into space. Coxhead was a brilliant international player who had broken a leg and been ordered by doctors to retire from football; it was a national disaster.

"Just like brothers," he said. "He used to live three streets away at home; we signed as amateurs for City together. He'd often be round at our house to have a meal, and whenever he's been playing in London, I've always gone round to see him. I've never missed. Like brothers." Suddenly he shot back the sleeve of his camel hair coat, rose out of his chair and said, "Look at this, I've got to go!"

I left him outside a tube station, where a cold, gusty wind blew across the deserted pavements, and the lighted mouth of the station seemed a warm cavern of refuge. What was he doing in London? Why did he stay? What strange *ignis fatuus* was he pursuing through the dark, unfriendly streets, the ugly stadiums, the dim hotels?

I could guess how he lived, and when one night I visited his lodgings, they did not surprise me. The house was semi-detached, with a shrivelled derisory apron of a garden, ghostly and hideous under the street lamp. He unlocked the front door and took me into a chill, cramped hallway; dark polished wooden bannisters and a steep narrow stairway led up into the dark. He switched on a light and showed me the dining-room, an unused room, crowded and over-furnished, with bookcases of encyclopaedias, gift sets of Dickens, mottled wallpaper and a long, shining mahogany table.

"They're nice here," he said contentedly, "They look after me well. Wait here and I'll be down." He went through the doorway and disappeared with long, agile strides up the stairs: he'd wanted to be a footballer but "just hadn't got it. They've asked me to play down here, you know, amateur, but you know how you get – I can't be bothered."

When he came down again, he was carrying a pile of cheap coloured exercise books. "Here you are," he said, thrusting them at me, "collected works. Now don't go pinching anything out of them, will you? I know you journalists! No, seriously, Brian," and his face became very serious indeed, "I'd like to know what you think. Only let me have them back as soon as you can, won't you, there's a good lad, because Charlie Pick of the *Mirror* says he'll have a look at them as well. I wouldn't mind joining the *Mirror*: plenty of scope for getting things off your chest. There's a lot wrong with football that ought to be put right, you know: I was talking to Danny Wilson of Fulham..."

I took the exercise books home and put them in a drawer. Peter rang within a week to ask me what I had thought of them, and I told him I was only halfway through. The next week he rang again and, with resignation, I took the books out, meaning to glance at them, then send them back. To my surprise, they were coherent and intelligent. They were written in a broad, clear hand with no margins and few paragraphs, but the arguments were convincing and well sustained, even though many of them raised echoes. I sent them back to him with an encouraging note: perhaps his ambitions had more basis, more hope of fulfilment, than it had seemed.

He did not answer my letter, and in the weeks which intervened before I saw him again, I heard people beginning to complain about him. They were journalists: what the footballers and managers thought of him was hard to tell: tight-grouped, they had about them a friendly yet excluding sufficiency. Now and again I could infer a rebuff: so-and-so was "getting big-headed. He's changing, you know, with all the publicity; it does it to some of them. The other City lads are saying so, too; ever since he played for England."

But the journalists made no bones about it. "One moment he isn't there," said the *Daily News*, "the next, there he is in the seat beside you."

On Saturday trains to the Midlands, he was sometimes half rebuffed. People answered his questions brusquely, empty seats were represented to him as taken, then remained empty, but he was not discouraged.

"Hey, every time I ring you up, your operator says you're out. I said, tell the bugger it's about time he stayed indoors and did some blooming work."

He hung on without effort, fluent and persuading, urgent about nothing, keeping his end up by the occasional suggested favour. Once, on the way back from a match at Birmingham, we were talking about suits; the *Mirror* and the *Express* were dressed to kill.

"Look, if you want suits," Peter said: he leaned across the table, pink and intense. "Any time you want one, honestly, Brian, George... Just come along with me, there's a pal of mine in Windmill Street; he'll make it up for you wholesale price. Come along and just let him give you a fitting; he'll quote you a figure." He begged and urged until it seemed that it was we who were doing him a favour, but when two of us turned up in Windmill Street the following Monday, he was not there.

"I didn't forget," he said, unworried, when next I met him. "I'll tell you what happened: you remember that County were in town for a Cup match? Well, my old pal Jackie was in the team, and afterwards we went out on the town, you know. I never got out of bed next day; I rang the bank and told them I'd got 'flu."

It was the last straw. People were avoiding him now; groups dissolved at his appearance; people were always out when he telephoned or called. When one met him, he seemed less sure of himself; his approach was made almost with circumspection. At Stamford Bridge one Saturday, I asked him, feeling sorry for him and a little guilty, how his journalistic career was going.

"Oh, that," he said, vaguely. "There might be a chance on the *Express*; Joe Butterfield was telling me."

"But I thought you said the *Daily Mail*..."

"No," he replied, detached and far away. "Joe Butterfield's got my books at the moment..."

And then it became plain to me that a humiliation was being prepared for him. Who would deliver it, where, what they would say, was unpredictable: it was simply in the air. He had forced the pace too hard, and Fleet Street resented him: the mention of his name, now, provoked a grimace and a groan, "You've seen his notebooks, haven't you? Well, you must be about the only one left who hasn't."

I wanted to warn him, but did not know how. Subtle hints were futile: his very stock in trade was his ability to ignore them. And, this being so, from what point did one start; what could be the preliminaries? Did one say bluntly, man-to-man, "Look here, all this hanging on of yours... people are getting a bit sick of it." Of course not; one could see already the wounded face, the look of hurt incomprehension.

No; Fate would have to overtake him; there was nothing to be done; one could only hope that when the rebuff came, it would not be too brutal. Instead, it was very brutal indeed. It was given, appropriately, in the dim-lighted corridor that runs outside the dressing-rooms at West Ham. It was featureless, flicked with the sharp tang of embrocation; a blind, imprisoning corridor without windows, closely guarded by a man on its door. But Peter had a way round all such men, and he already stood blandly among a little group of journalists which waited to be let into the dressing-rooms; stood, slightly and appositely, on the fringe, the token of his waning confidence. He was saying, "I wonder whether I can get in... I told Ted I was here," but the journalists were talking among themselves, paying him no attention.

"I haven't seen him for months," he tried again, throwing out the words like bait to a fish. "We were on a course together, once..."

Boldly – desperately, perhaps – he stepped forward into the very middle of the group, laying a quick hand on the fat shoulder of Wilf Rigby, of the *Gazette*. "Wilf," he said, "if I can't get in, will you take him a message..."

The red, jowled, drinker's face pivoted on its thick red neck. Rigby was a loud, uncertain bull, roaring to keep his spirits up, trampling without real malice on fact and other people's opinions, timid as a girl in print.

"For Christ's sake," he said, "what do you want now? Why can't you bloody well let us alone when you can see we're doing our job? You butt in where nobody wants you, you get in the way when we're trying to have interviews. Why don't you go back to your bank instead of poncing on the boys for tickets and hanging round us?"

While he spoke, Peter's face was swept by misery and astonishment. His jaw had fallen open in sheer unbelief; the pale eyes goggled out appalled from behind his spectacles, while the rest of us looked away, shuffled our feet, talked quickly and tried to detach ourselves from the scene.

He was still standing frozen in the corridor when the dressing-room door opened, to a waft of steam and embrocation, and we were allowed to file in.

That was the end of him, then. I was at once sorry and relieved, glad to be rid of an incubus, sorry for the cruel way it had been done. I began uneasily recalling his goodwill, his lonely innocence, his moments of generosity.

The following week, there was an important match at Tottenham, and I arrived early, realising with a shock, as I passed the touts, that Peter wasn't there. In the car park, Rigby had arrived early too, and was talking to a player; his voice bellowed out, didactic and uncompromising; my first reaction was to avoid him, but I wanted to talk to the player, and joined them.

Others joined us in turn, until at length the player made his apologies and went in to change. It was then, advancing from a far corner of the desolate car park, that I saw the camel hair coat. It was he – there was no doubt of it, whatever the incredibility of his presence – advancing quickly, not sheering off but making straight towards us. Rigby saw him, too, bent upon him his hostile and insensitive stare, and opened and shut his mouth, without speaking.

Then he himself was on us, affable and bland. "Hello, John, hello, Wilf, hello Brian. Hey, have you seen Jimmy Watson? He promised me there'd be a ticket."

The prodigy

The notebooks stood in a pile on top of the glass-fronted cabinet, in the little dining-room. Seeing them I asked Franco if they were records of his team, his young footballers.

"*Ma, no!*" he said, blond head bent over his plate, his huge, bare forearms spread across the table, "*ma no!*" and he gave one of his muted and surprising smiles, private and enigmatic, the volcano at rest.

"It's a Fascist," he said, stuffing cheese into his mouth. "He wants me to take on his son."

"And will you?"

"*Ma!*" A shrug; again, the private smile. "Perhaps. I don't know."

Franco was famous, now; his young protégés, found in the streets and squares of Florence, in little teams run by local priests, were transmuted by him into League footballers, a fortune in their feet. Franco was the alchemist, his crucible the bumpy little ground in Rifredi, where he put them through their paces among the factories, and the myriad, chemical smells.

"Afterwards I'll show you," he said, and his voice took on a new tone – reluctant admiration – though the smile remained, "he's written up everything; from the very beginning" – and from the top of the table, his father rumblingly concurred. "*Tutto!*" he said, his head rising massively above his newspaper, *L'Avanti! "ha scritto tutto!"*

His wife – Franco's stepmother – hovered like a kind ghost above us. "*Mangia, mangia!* Don't you like cheese?"

"Of course I do," I said.

The notebooks were long, beige covered, with a red binding. Opening the one on top, I found each page as carefully plotted as a garden. There were snapshots, letters, here and there a newspaper cutting; above all, the record, the commentary, now written in a firm yet flowery running-hand, now typed on sheets of foolscap which had been pasted in.

"When Piero reached his second birthday, I began his training; at first, very gentle running, three times round the room, without a pause, the exercise itself repeated four times. After he had twice run round the room, he wanted to stop, and I was forced to punish him. He cried, but then resumed the exercise, which he was able to complete. Without discipline, it is impossible to make an athlete. I am convinced that only in this way can one be *certain* of producing an outstanding footballer."

I turned over several pages. "When Piero was four, I began a further exercise, which I had also carefully devised; that of running up and down stairs. On the first day, I obliged him to do it only twice, with a pause of exactly two minutes between the first completed exercise and the second. He complained of feeling out of breath, so that on the second day, instead of increasing it to four, I increased it only to three. By the end of the week, however, he had succeeded in reaching my original target of six consecutive exercises, performed with a break of only twenty-five seconds between each. We are making good progress."

I was at grips with an obsession. Through page after page, notebook after notebook, the voice droned in my ear, changeless and inexorable, humourless, determined, bitterly proud, till one wanted to cry out for the child who was the victim of its pride – running round the room, running upstairs, forced to do ten press-ups, twenty press-ups, to kick a ball a hundred times against a wall, to trap it fifty times, without a fault.

"And he's a Fascist?" I asked, looking up; but the question was rhetorical. In their pride, their humourless vanity, their lurking sentimentalism, their philosophy of pointless sacrifice, the notebooks distilled the very quintessence of Fascism.

I took up another volume, and another, while the old man, scepticism gone, grinned and chuckled at the television, as though it were an indulged and favourite grandchild. Franco, meanwhile, strode to and from the clamouring telephone, bellowing advice to his pupils in his thick, Tuscan accent. *"Allora, non gioca!* Don't play! Don't even train! Tomorrow I'll take you to the clinic, and we'll get some heat on it!"

The notebooks proceeded through schooldays, through the first organized games of football: "One saw clearly that Piero was already a disciplined and dedicated player; this by contrast with the others, who were still children, merely enjoying themselves." Poor little Piero.

"How old is he now? " I asked Franco.

"How old?" repeated Franco, moving in his heavy, restless, shuffling, distracted way about the room. *"Quel bischero lì?* He's just turned sixteen."

I opened still another notebook, and this time the boy himself appeared in a team group – a boy indeed, dwarfed, ludicrously small – round faced and precocious, smiling confidently at the camera, his hair slicked and brillian-tined like a professional's. Perhaps he did have talent; how else could he hold his own among players so much bigger? The commentary, indeed, made him the star, the scorer of goals, the young matador.

"We now come," I read, "to a disgrace, a shameful event, a match which it is painful to describe. Piero's team, Rondinella di Cascine, was to play San Antonio. It was agreed before the match that Rondinella would concede a penalty and lose, San Antonio being in fear of relegation. When Piero heard of this, he pleaded with Bandini, the coach, but to no avail. Ten minutes from the end, when there was still no score, Bandini gave a signal and his son, the left-back, handled deliberately in his own penalty area; the only one capable of such a thing. Nothing to be done. A penalty. A shot – and a goal. Piero came off the field weeping. 'Why didn't they pass the ball to me?' he said. 'I would have equalised.'"

He was a centre-forward; it seemed inevitable: the focal position, where goals were to be scored, glory to be won.

Franco leaned over my shoulder, striking the notebook with a heavy, scornful hand. *"Ma!"* he said. *"Roba da pazzi!* Crazy!" and then, in his unique English, "Come with me tomorrow to Rifredi: I make you see my team. Lovely young *players!* I have a right-half of '45, already he is one metre, eighty. Like an English player! You have no idea!"

I came on him by chance, a few days later, in the portico, beside the newspaper kiosk which was at once his landmark and his rendezvous. *"Ha-*llo my *dear!"* he cried, arms outstretched in salutation and delight. Around him stood his usual band of satellites, the tall, plump, grey-haired man who drew diagrams of play, and drank; the curly headed steward, from the Fiorentina stadium; the retarded boy, a faithful dog, who followed Franco everywhere, hoping for bones, and eyed me now with wary resentment.

"Come with me Sunday!" bellowed Franco. "You will see my team! They are playing at Scarperia!"

"Will Piero be playing?"

"Macche Piero? Oh!" he cried, and went into a pantomime of laughter, bent double, slapping his thighs and knees. "Avanzolini's son!" he told the group. "That Fascist journalist... the little boy."

"So he won't play?"

"He may do," said Franco, in Italian – calm again, shrugging his wide shoulders. "It's only a friendly game. Perhaps I'll give him a trial."

"What sort of player is he?" asked the newsagent, grave among his papers and his lurid paperbacks.

Franco shrugged again. *"Cosa vuoi?* Too small. He hasn't got the energy. All this running up and down the stairs, when he was a child..."

We went by coach to Scarperia, the radio, the inevitable radio, blaring incessant dance music; but Franco's roar could be heard above it all, as he strode up and down among his players, counselling and jesting.

"This one is my inside-right: he is a blockhead!"

Piero sat quietly with his father, at the back of the coach. I recognised immediately the round, immature face beneath the brilliantined hair, though it was at once older and more thoughtful than in the photograph. I almost felt that I would have recognised his father, too; a sombre, desiccated man, brown skinned, hollow cheeked, the mouth tight, his rich, wavy black hair as carefully combed as his son's. Franco introduced me to them – *"grande esperto calcistico inglese,"* the great English football expert, with that flamboyance which always made me feel a sham.

"Piacere," Avanzolini said rising from his seat, his thin hand clasping mine in a pincer grip. "I, too, am a journalist."

The boy responded shyly, with unexpected courtesy.

The cares of the world seemed to rest on his shoulders; he might have been playing for his life.

"I must be honest," Avanzolini said. "I'm not for the English. I'm a Fascist."

"Enough of this Fascism!" roared Franco, a Socialist like his father.

"No, no," pursued the journalist, "you must let me explain. Although I'm not pro-English, there are many English things that I admire; for instance, English football. The English player is a real professional; I'm always saying so to Piero."

The coach's horn blared, and blared again, as we swept around a narrow mountain corner. We were in the very heart of Tuscany now; above us, on either side, rose the pale, grey-green sweep of olive trees, tier upon tier of them, perfect and precise. What had all this to do with football? Were we not desecrating it, with our vulgar purpose, and our noise?

"Will he play?" the journalist asked Franco, suddenly, his lean face rigid with suspense.

"It depends, it depends," said Franco, vaguely, while the boy looked out of the window, as if he couldn't hear.

"A friendly match," said the journalist. "At least for the second half... You could see what he's capable of doing..."

The Scarperia ground lay high on the top of a hill; around it, incongruously, stood the high, wire "safety netting" associated with Italian League
grounds, where passions boil and crowds must be deterred. It was early May,
and a bland sun played over the bumpy little pitch, over the olive trees on
slopes around us and below us, so that we, the ground, the few spectators,
standing round the netting, seemed to have intruded somehow into the
landscape of a *cinquecento* painting.

The game was a bad one, the light ball bedevilled by the pitch. Franco's
boys played in red, with a sort of weary expertise; they weren't coming off,
but there was something in their attitude, their self-possession, which
suggested that they might on another day. As the match unwound its slow
course, Franco prowled restlessly around the touchline, shirt-sleeved, his
jacket slung, characteristically, over his shoulder, now thundering at his
team, now turning to roar at the spectators. "*Ma giocano come bischeri!*" he
cried. "*Macche, the ti tiri una sega?*" This, to his outside-left, who turned, at
the obscenity, and grinned. Franco's face, with its great, prowed nose, was
pinked by the sun. He passed beside me, chuckling, resting a hand on my
shoulder, "You have not seen me train my players. I beat them, I club them!
You have no idea!"

Ten yards away from us, tautly attentive to the game, stood the slow boy;
each time Franco passed, he turned urgently to speak to him, Franco
answering with a shrug or a bantering word. Once I approached him, to ask
what League the Scarperia team belonged to, but he answered, sullenly, "*Chi
lo sa?* Who knows?" and returned to his tense observation.

Further still down the touchline stood the journalist and his son. I strolled
past them; they were looking on in silence, Avanzolini with an aquiline
fierceness, as if he were willing someone to be hurt, and leave the field; or, if
they remained, to play badly. As for the boy, he watched sadly, like an invalid,
envying his playmates. Franco prowled by, and the journalist stopped him,
but Franco's mouth turned up at the corner, his eyebrows rose. "We'll see," I
heard him say, "we'll see."

At last the referee blew his whistle for half-time, and Franco sauntered on
to the pitch, to address his team. I looked again at the journalist; his eyes
were fixed on Franco, he was craning forward like some beast about to
spring, compelling him, by sympathetic magic. But Franco was impervious;
he stood among his team, his great arms gesturing, hugging one player,
contemptuously pushing another, and I felt for the journalist and the boy,
hanging in limbo: till suddenly they were released, as Franco turned,

signalling, with a cry of, *"Va bene, gioca, gioca,"* and his centre-forward came off the field, peeling his shirt over his head, throwing it to Piero.

Still Avanzolini did not smile, but his tight mouth drew wider with satisfaction, while the boy, catching the shirt, looked up at him with a start of joy. Then he ran to the gate in the wire, disappeared past a curtain of trees, and returned three minutes later, still running, now fully changed.

Franco's team kicked off, to begin the second half, so that the boy, as centre-forward, touched the ball at once, tapping it to his inside-right, rushing eagerly forward for a return pass, as though he were determined to burst the battle-line alone. But the inside-right, callous and lethargic, turned casually away, flicking the ball back, instead, to his wing-half, so that the boy, like some tiny, horseless Quixote, was left galloping bravely into nowhere.

And this set the pattern of his game; he was out of rhythm and sympathy with the others, they played in waltz time, while his was the tempo of a samba. He was too keen to do well, forever chasing, arriving fractionally too late, a devoted follower of lost causes. There was his size, too, making each enterprise doubly difficult. He could not force his way through, but must always resort to pace and guile. Once, he was knocked flying, landing with a cruel thud on the hard, abrasive ground, while his father yelled in protest from the touchline: *"Fallo! Che scorrettismo!"* One of his bigger team-mates lugged him nonchalantly to his feet; his knee was bleeding, but he waved the solicitous referee away, limped a few paces and played on.

As he ran and leaped and tumbled, I found myself identifying with him, hoping that at least he could score; a goal – with its unique, ecstatic moment of triumph – could redeem him. He was trying much too hard and, inevitably, making mistakes, misplacing passes, shooting over the bar, to the spectators' howls, letting the ball bounce out of his control.

Along the touchline, a trail of cigarette butts marked his father's progress. Now, when Franco passed him, he did not turn round, as though afraid of what he might hear. But I, without his involvement, did ask Franco what he thought, and he replied, with the inevitable shrug, *"Così piccolo; c'è poco da fare.* So small; there's not much to be done."

"But there've been good little centre-forwards," I said, to receive another shrug, implying that these had genius, while this... I hoped he was not right, but was afraid he might be; by the end of the game, there was nothing to fall back on but excuses; on another day, in other circumstances, with another, more familiar team...

On the journey back, the radio blared at us again, but now, after the effort of the match, the boys were silent and relaxed, as though in sympathy with the failing day, the twilight gathering outside over rocks and slopes and olive trees. No one spoke to the journalist and his son. They sat where they had sat before, apart, but this time, the journalist was talking, quietly and incessantly, his thin hands moving in short, dynamic gestures as he made each point. His son followed him, wide-eyed; I thought I could see tears on his cheeks. I wished Franco would go up to him and say some word of comfort, but he sprawled in his seat, seemingly unaware, now and again shouting to a player, gaining a laugh.

When the bus stopped in Rifredi, and we all got out, the journalist came up to Franco; I heard him say, "He can play better than this, I swear to you. He deserves another chance," to which Franco nodded in his vague, distracted way, replying, "All right; we'll see, we'll see." The journalist turned to me, extending his hand, saying, with great formality, *"Molto lieto,"* like a proud man who has publicly disgraced himself, but won't show that he knows it. The boy's farewell was shamefaced; he would hardly meet my eye.

I watched them disappear down the road, the journalist inclining towards his son, already talking, counselling. I felt as sorry for one, now, as the other.

Soon after this, I returned to England, and it was a year before I was in Florence again. I went to dinner with Franco; he was as full as ever of his protégés; as always, last year's prodigies were "blockheads... *bischeracci";* he had others, who were twice as good.

"And what about Piero?" I asked. "The little one whose father taught him."

"I make a trial of him with Bologna," Franco said, and gave his strange, muted smile, as if to say that the vagaries of professional clubs were beyond him.

"Do you think they'll sign him?"

"Maybe."

I was intrigued – Bologna were a famous club – but he would tell me no more. One afternoon, however, walking through Piazza della Repubblica, I saw Piero and his father, sitting at a cafe table, and approached them. Both rose at once to their feet. The journalist did not smile, but his profession of pleasure now seemed more than formal, even if I suspected he was pleased for his own sake, rather than mine; that my function was to admire. The boy had grown; he was as tall, now, as his father, and his face had lost its chubby adolescence. In his open-necked blue jersey and his blue jeans, he suggested a new maturity. Behind his courtesy lay, no longer timidity, but the alert assurance of the young Italian male.

I sat down with them, and his father insisted on ordering me a cognac, though I wanted coffee. "Tomorrow," he said, "Piero has a trial with Bologna."

"I know," I said. "I wish him luck."

The boy thanked me, with a return of his old diffidence.

"Excuse me," said his father, leaning across the little table, "but he doesn't need luck. He's certain to succeed."

"Well, yes," I said. "Franco's a marvellous coach."

"Excuse me," he said again, his eyes searching mine like a hypnotist's. "I'm always frank. I esteem Signor Angiolini. He's a good coach, there's no doubt about it. But he's only taken Piero late in his development, at a time when any good coach would get the same result. The important work was done already." He paused, then looking past my ear, with careful detachment said, "It was done by me."

"I know," I told him, flatly.

"*How* do you know?" he snapped, and whirled back to me again, a child in his disappointment.

"Franco told me."

"Did he tell you how I began when he was two years old? Did he tell you how I planned every step of his development?"

"Yes," I said.

I glanced at the boy, but his face showed nothing; he'd withdrawn from the conversation, as if it had nothing to do with him, and was gazing out across the square. There was another, small hiatus, then Avanzolini said, less arrogant now than defiant, even sullen, "You'll see; he'll become a great champion."

"I hope he will," I said.

But I didn't think he would; it was too long a shot, however much he had improved. Even if he came through his trial with Bologna, there were a thousand obstacles in the way; temperament, fortune, injury; life in a floodlit and frenetic goldfish bowl. He might stay with Bologna for a season, then be transferred to some wretched little Sicilian club, whose players slept three in a room and were paid, if they were lucky, months in arrears.

Yet there was more to it than that. Though I liked the boy, I was half aware I did not want him to succeed, just as I felt that Franco, too, grudged his success: he, because he must forever share the credit, I, because the father's hubris repelled me. How could he succeed? There was a blasphemy about it all.

Before I left Florence, I heard that the boy had passed his trial. "They took him on," Franco told me, with his enigmatic smile; he seemed half-impressed, half-sceptical.

"Are you surprised? "

"Ma," he said. *"Va discretamente bene.* He isn't doing badly."

I once more returned to London, and thought little about the boy till winter when, opening the Italian football weekly which I read, I was confronted by his name: SI CHIAMA AVANZOLINI LA NUOVA PRO MESSA DEL BOLOGNA: Bologna's new hope is called Avanzolini.

He had just made his League debut for them in a home match against Juventus, scoring two goals, one of them the winner. There were photographs of each of them, another of the boy, head bowed, walking beside a lean, solicitous man in a light raincoat and a flat-brimmed hat, who had an arm around his shoulder: "Avanzolini weeps with joy as he leaves the field, accompanied by his manager." I looked in vain for another photograph; Avanzolini with his father. The journalist would not be crying, I was sure of that; he would be wearing an expression of Luciferan triumph.

Nor was Piero a nine days' wonder; he kept his place, continuing to score goals; the sure way to the heart of the Italian football public. In due time, the magazine published an article about him, and now the photograph of his father did appear, a hand on the boy's shoulder, but this hand restraining, proprietorial, the eyes staring, not at the boy, but exultantly, straight into the camera. Each week, when the magazine arrived, I looked immediately for Piero's name, and each week, I was not disappointed. Towards the end of the season, the Italian Under 23 team was due to meet England, in Birmingham, and I found myself hoping he'd be chosen. He was, indeed, picked for the trial games and then to my pleasure, for the actual team.

I travelled to Birmingham to see the game. It was played beneath the cold, steep, wind-swept terraces, the absurd, red brick neo-Gothic, of Villa Park. More absurd still was the thought of seeing Piero in this context. As he came on to the field, a sturdy, even heavy, figure in his blue jersey, perfectly at ease, a professional among professionals, I thought of his Calvary on the bumpy little ground of Scarperia. Where was his father? Somewhere in the crowd, I supposed; no doubt I should see both of them, when the game was done.

It must have been nearly ten minutes before the ball first came to Piero. He was in the English penalty area, his back to goal, and at once he kicked himself off the ground with one foot, flicked the ball over his head with the other, still in mid air; the *rovesciata*, good for applause on any ground in Italy. The ball flew over the bar, and the English crowd went, *"Ooooh..."* in a great, collective sigh of amazed relief.

In that moment, I knew his father had succeeded – a new Pygmalion – it didn't need the later evidence of virtuosity, the swerve with which he tricked the English centre-half, the goal he headed from a corner, the balls he effortlessly killed, at any height and pace. Once again, his father's face rose in front of me, stiff with satisfaction – as it must be looking, somewhere in the stand.

Afterwards, I went down to the Italian dressing-room, full of steam and chattering, naked men. Piero himself stood half nude, wearing only his blue, international jersey. He greeted me eagerly, with controlled surprise, modestly receiving my congratulations.

"And your father?" I asked.

"He didn't come," he answered with a shrug, and his smile vanished.

"Couldn't he manage it?" Again he shrugged, now with a certain embarrassment, and said, "You know how it is... sons... fathers."

And with these words, that moment, I did know how it was, knew the perfect pattern of it all.

There was no need to see the journalist again, but I did see him, the following May – in Florence once more – crossing the Pante Vecchio, where the blue haired old American women clamoured at the trinket shops. He would have passed me, but I stopped him. He was thinner than ever and in his face, satisfaction had given way to total bitterness; his pride, now, lay in what had been done to him.

Before I could stop myself, I had said, "I saw your son in Birmingham," and he gave the first smile I'd ever seen from him, as though he welcomed this new wound.

"*Oggi, la gioventu...*" he said. "Youth today; it's another generation. Gratitude doesn't exist, there's no discipline. When a young man succeeds, he owes something to people who've helped him, to his parents, his teachers. He should live a simple life; no girls, no motor cars... I must be honest: I know you're English, but in the time of Fascism, these things wouldn't have been possible."

I could not meet his eyes. I looked past his shoulder and, across the road at the end of the bridge, I saw a newspaper bill, in red, white and black... "Avanzolini chosen again for the national team." Then the thin, hard hand was shaking mine, and he was walking down the bridge, across the road, past the bill, without a pause. But I knew that he had seen it.

All Rovers fans

On the dingy station platform, among the clamour and commotion of the fans, the chants and shouts, the sudden, swift incursions of police, the guffaws and the obscenities, the man and the boy formed a small, still island of intensity. Both were Rovers fans; otherwise, there seemed no meeting point. The man, who was talking quickly, eagerly, as the boy listened, his face alive with the passion of his discourse, was squat and rough. There was an aura about him of park benches, doss houses, even prisons. Heavy shouldered, he wore a shiny, cheap blue suit, a white shirt open at the neck, although the day was cold. His hair, thick, black and oiled, hung to well below his collar. In this enthusiasm, he did not seem aware that the boy was regarding him with a certain slight unease.

He was about sixteen, a plump boy with a soft, dark, Jewish face. If the man appeared used to be roughing it, the boy looked manifestly pampered. When the train eventually drew into London, he would surely go back to a warm home with fitted carpets, a mother who sat him down to a substantial dinner, while the man would go God knows where – to some squalid rooming house, to a Salvation Army shelter?

Still, they talked. The thickset man was saying, "That's him, though, innit? Don't see him half the game, forget he's even there, then wallop, goal! Like he done today."

"Yeah, he's good like that," said the boy.

"He's good, yes, he's good, but he's entitled to be better. With the talent he got, he should be better."

Both spoke with London accents, but where the man's was the thick, slurred, glottal Cockney of the East End, the boy's, higher pitched, had the slightly nasal overlay of Stamford Hill, or perhaps, stepping westward, Golders Green.

All about them, as the football excursion train came gliding to the platform, swirled skinheads, with their brutal crops, their braces worn over coloured tee-shirts, their thick, heavy, threatening boots; burly youths in jean jackets, scarves dangling from their wrists, a small, gold earring in their right ears; even punks with jagged hair dyed green and purple. The boy's eyes flickered anxiously about him as the crowd rushed past, charged the carriages, wrenched open doors, fought to get through them.

"Come on!" the man said, "*there's* one!", and went dashing down the platform with the boy behind him, now dodging, now bumping and buffetting, reaching a carriage farther down the train, forcing his way through the scrum of people, up the steps, into the carriage, the boy still following in his wake, till they were sitting opposite each other, panting, smiling, in a long, open, second-class compartment.

"Gotta be quick, haven't you?" the man said. "Gotta be decisive! Like football. Like in the penalty area, innit?" The boy smiled back and nodded.

They sat in the window seats. Beside them were two other fans, one a middle aged man with bushy grey hair and a woollen cap in the club's blue and white colours, the other a tall, thin, fair-haired boy, the club's scarf around his neck.

"Fucking showed 'em, didn't we?" said the man.

As the passengers settled down, as seats were found, the wandering began. Up and down the train went the young fans, shouting, jostling, drinking beer out of cans, hoarse and raucous, chanting their monotonous dirge of "*Rovers, Rovers!*", swopping their tales of violence and conquest.

"Twenty of 'em there when we got to the station. Geezer with a bottle, another with a bleedin' flick knife. Nutted one, put the boot in another."

"Old Bill came steaming in, sorted a few out. Old Terry, 'e got done again."

Then another chant:

"We 'ate Arsenal!

We 'ate Arsenal!"

From all this frantic, motiveless activity, the man and the boy were detached; the man too old to be a part of it, the boy disinclined by nature.

"Don't come for the game, that lot," said the man, and they exchanged another smile.

"Follow them everywhere, do you?" asked the man.

"Not everywhere," the boy said. "Quite a lot."

"Up to Middlesbrough, places like that?"

"Well... sometimes."

He was still wary. If the fans were not his kind, then neither was the man, who brought into his warm, protected world a harsh breath of the outside. Now and again, as the fans pushed by in their lemming progress, the man exchanged a joke with them. The boy did not speak to them at all; he seemed to shrink physically away from them into his corner. Their scarves, their crops, their earrings and tattoos, their heavy boots, made his own neat, blue anorak, his polished shoes, seem bourgeois and effete.

"Don't your parents like you going?" the man asked, suddenly. It was the first suggestion that there might be barriers between them, that the boy came from another, gentler scene.

"Not much," the boy mumbled, eyes upon the grubby floor.

"Live in London, do you?"

"Yes."

"Whereabouts?"

"Willesden."

"Nice there, is it?"

"All right. Where do... *you* live?"

"Round about," the man said. "Here and there. Always supported Rovers. Have you?"

"Yes."

"Same here."

"We 'ate Arsenal!" chanted a bunch of fans marching past.

As the journey wore on, as the beer flowed from the cans, the tone became harsher and more menacing. There was an edge of violence to it now, as if the fans were seeking prey.

"We 'ate Villa!"

The team had just beaten Aston Villa.

"Any Villa fans 'ere? Any Villa fans 'iding 'ere?"

"We all agree,

Aston Villa are wankers!"

The man grinned at this, then smiled across at the boy, whose own smile was a grimace.

"Wouldn't get *this* train, would they?" asked the man. "Not Villa fans."

Each fresh wave of supporters was more aggressive than the one before.

"We 'ate niggers!" came the new chant. "We 'ate niggers!"

"Ain't seen none on *this* train," said the man. "Just as well, I reckon."

"Yes," said the boy, less and less audible. He seemed to be expecting some catastrophe. The man looked at him with quizzical surprise, then turned to talk to the older fan beside him.

"Marvellous shot he's got on him, that Ronnie."

From the next carriage, a cry floated back, "Kill the yids!" and now the boy visibly stiffened, seemed to shrink still further into his seat, looking out with desperate intensity at the smooth, green, sloping pasture land that sped by the window.

"Kill the yids!" came more faintly back down the train. The tone was almost jocular, but the boy now bent his whole body round and away from the carriage behind him, his study of the fields outside now so obsessive that it might have been that of a botanist. It was as if he wanted to convince himself that only the fields, the countryside, were real; that the train and its passengers no longer existed.

Now they were coming again.

"The yids, the yids!"

"We gotta get rid of the yids!"

"*Sieg Heil! Sieg Heil!*"

The boy cowered at the window. The man ceased talking for a moment to glance at him, and grin. Down the train and back, now the youths were singing, to the tune of a pop song: "We are *Na*-zis, we are *Na*-zis!"

As they came into the carriage, there were about a dozen of them, most of them skinheads, some in jean jackets, all wearing the inevitable boots. When they and their noise had disappeared again, the boy at last looked timidly round, to find the man smiling at him.

"You one?" he asked. The boy looked at him, petrified, then, almost imperceptibly, he nodded. The man continued gazing at him, smiling, without speaking. He seemed amused, almost pleased. At last he said, "I wouldn't worry. Songs, that's all it is."

The boy swallowed, gave another nod, and followed it with the sickly parody of a smile.

"Just songs and that," the man said.

The boy turned back to the refuge of the window. The man went on looking at him, smiling for a while, then resumed his conversation with the other fan.

"Mind you," he said, "I reckon that he likes a pint, old Ronnie. People I know seen him up the Nag's Head."

The shouts and chants had ceased now, but the fans would be back; mindlessly, restlessly, ceaselessly in motion, looking for excitement, violence, victims.

The boy turned from the window again, pulled the programme of the match out of his pocket, and began to read it as though he were committing it to memory.

"Collect 'em, do you?" asked the man.

The boy said, "Yes," the merest motion of the lips.

"I collected them, and all, when I was your age," said the man, the smile still on his face. "The trouble is, they kept on getting nicked. People would pinch them."

The boy gave a grimace of response, then resumed his tense study of the programme.

"They're different now, of course," the man said. "Bigger, lot more pictures. More expensive." "Something to read," said the older fan. "Something to do while you're waiting."

"Ever win the Lucky Programme?" asked the man. "I had one once. Don't know where it was. Somewhere up north – Huddersfield, or somewhere. Years ago. I got a quid – that's all I got, a quid. The Lucky Programme. Kind of luck I've always had."

The boy did not look up. Now the voices could be heard again.

"'E's only a poor little Scouser,
'Is face is tattered and torn.
'E made me feel sick,
So I gave 'im a brick,
And now 'e don't sing any more."

As the sound grew nearer, the boy put down his programme and met the man's smiling face in a fleeting, anguished look of appeal, before turning back to the window.

"Kill the yids!" cried the voices. "Kill the yids!"

The fans were in the carriage now, they were approaching, they were level, they had stopped.

"Any yids in here?" a voice asked. " Oo's 'e? What's 'e doing, looking out like that?"

"Looks like a yid."

The boy did not move. Rigid, he went on staring out of the window as the fields rushed past, a haze of green.

At last, he heard the man speak: "He's a Rovers fan, isn't 'e? 'E's Rovers."

"Thought he was a yid," a voice said. "*Looks* like one."

"Nah," said the man, " 'e's Rovers," and the boots moved off.

"We '*ate* Arsenal!"

"We '*ate* Arsenal!"

The boy turned slowly from the window. His body shook, his mouth was trembling. "All Rovers fans, aren't we?" said the man, and winked at him.

The thing he loves

How did it *feel*, John?
It felt terrible. The worst moment in my life. Terrible, it felt. It still does.

It always will. It's going to be with me forever, this; the moment. Sleeping and waking. Dreaming about it. Then waking up, remembering about it. Through the windscreen, out of the pelting rain, suddenly this figure rushing. And thinking these two things, me: or rather one thing, and under it another.

First, bloody hell, he's mad, what's he doing? And under it, right in the same split second, a sort of, somehow, *recognising*. But all of it happening so quick; bang on the footbrake, then that dreadful bump. Oh, Christ, I've hit him. Getting out of the car, all shaking, then seeing him there, his body, and the shock again, this time the double shock, the body and the blood. Slumped over, with his back to me. And then the other feeling, stronger, suddenly, recognising. God, please God, don't let it, don't let it be him, it can't be him. And sort of hearing people's voices: "Joe... It's Joey Black... Joe's dead... He's killed Joey." Then click: passing out.

Coming round, there was this big policeman, holding me. Rain in my face. "What happened, son?" And the voices, again: "It's Joey Black... Dead... Joey... Saw it all; he run out like a lunatic... Ay, but he could've stopped."

I said, "Is that right? Have I killed Joey Black?" And him, "All right, keep back, you lot. Now, what exactly happened, son?"

I asked him, "Is he *dead*? You've got to tell me, is he dead?" I think I went a bit hysterical, struggling away from him, standing up, trying to get over and see the body, but he stopped me, he hauled me back, I could just see all that mass of long fair hair, the blood around, then an ambulance came jangling up, folk scattering. They jumped out, threw a blanket over, and lifted him on a stretcher, then aboard, away, jangling. He was gone. Nothing in the road now but this patch of blood, washing away fast in the rain, disappearing in the gutter.

I said, "It *was* Joe, wasn't it, and he's dead." He said, "Ay, son, I'm afraid so," and it swept over me again, this faintness, but I shook it off, I fought it. In fact this was it; the worst moment in my life, because it was empty now, my life was, completely empty, nothing left of it, like they'd scooped me out inside and left the shell of me. I said, "It *can't* be," though I knew by now it was, it just *seemed* so impossible, seeing him play that very afternoon, just a few hours before. Him; and me, that worshipped him, that lived to see him play, that would have given myself in his place, any day.

They took me home in a police car. I walked through the door, a copper on either side of me; my mother's face, she couldn't understand it; I'd never been in trouble in me life.

I said, "I've killed him; Joey Black," not thinking what I said, and she tottered, then one of the coppers said, "A motor accident, it was; Market Square," and they put me to bed. I lay there, not ever wanting to get up again.

Has it changed your life in any way, John?
It *has* changed my life. It's changed it in a lot of ways.

One way it changed it, right from the first, was that it wasn't worth living, now. How could I face things? How was I going to face people?

Waking that first morning. Something black weighing on me, crushing me down. Remembering it, then. Snapping on the light above my bed, and seeing *him* looking straight at me from across the room, the lifesize photo of him in the City colours. And wherever I turned, to whichever wall, everywhere, there he was, staring at me, head and shoulders, action shots, or from out of a team group. Sometimes with long hair, sometimes with it shorter, from his early days, when he just got in the team. It was worse than anywhere, my room was, the accident came back and back to me, the rain, him running, then the thump, his body, till I hurried out into the bathroom, and I locked myself in there.

It was still early, only six o'clock. I stayed in there an hour or so, trying not to think about the accident, but if it wasn't the accident it was still him, Joey, running like he always used to run, shirt outside his shorts, the long hair flapping, dodging and swerving in the way he had, swaying over the ball, or sometimes scoring. The last goal he got – *that* came back to me – the one on Saturday, because it *was* the last; he'd never get another. I'd done for him.

I sat there: I was paralysed. I couldn't go out anywhere, I couldn't stay in. If I went out, they'd all be staring at me; it was bound to be in the papers by now. There he is, that's him, the one that killed Joe Black. And whatever I told them – I'm a City fan, I idolised him, I admired him as much as you ever did – none of that would make tuppence worth of difference, none of it could alter what I'd done, even if I never meant it.

But if I stayed home, in my room, there it all was, the dozens of reminders. I went back in there, thinking that I'd take them down, and the first thing I went to was the lifesize photo. I started unpinning it, to put it somewhere, then I stopped; I couldn't go on. His face was smiling at me, and I found I was seeing two things at once, not just the cardboard photo but his actual body, sprawled like it had been in the road.

I sat down on the bed and didn't move; I don't know how long I'd been there when my mother came in. She was in her dressing-gown, she'd brought a cup of tea, she said, "You couldn't help it, John," and then I started crying, it seemed to touch something off. I said, "I know I couldn't, I know I couldn't," tears all running down my face. I couldn't take the tea from her. I said, "Suddenly bang: like that. From nowhere. Right in front of me."

She said, "I know, I know, the policeman said it wasn't *your* fault."

I said, "But it *was* my fault. I was driving, wasn't I? It was my car wasn't it? It was me hit him, didn't I?"

She said, "If it hadn't been you, it would have been the next car."

I said, "What next car? Why should it? He'd have got across, he'd have been safe, he'd be alive to play."

Which set me off thinking about my car; a 1960 Morris Oxford it was that I'd picked up for a hundred quid and been so proud of; that I'd worked and worked on, God knows how many hours, stripping down the engine, fitting new parts until I think the whole damn thing must have been new, and all for this, this one moment in the Market Square.

When the old man came in later on and told me that the police had phoned, I could pick up the car on Monday from where it was in the pound, I said, "Leave it there. I never want to see it again."

He said, "Your *car?*" like he couldn't believe it. I said, "It's not my bloody car," and I thought of it sitting there in the police pound with, and this was the worst thing, the blue City sticker on its back window and the little blue City doll that hung in the windscreen, then of the dent there'd be in the front wing, maybe the bumper, and what that meant. I knew I could never drive that car again. I didn't think I'd ever *drive* again, come to that.

He stood there, the old man, looking at me, not talking, till in the end he asked me, "Are you going to work tomorrow?" I said: "No." He said, "You can't sit here the rest of your life." I said, "Leave me alone." He said, "Your breakfast's waiting on the table." I said, "Just leave me alone."

Wasn't Joey Black your favourite player, John?
He was everybody's favourite player, wasn't he?

Every City fan's; and lots that weren't City fans. There'll never be another like him. The goals he scored, the way he could go past people. A goal he got against the Arsenal; he must have gone round four defenders, all of them trying to chop him down, him swaying and swerving; inside one, outside the next, then when it looked like he was right off balance, shooting with the near foot as he fell, instead of bringing through the back foot, right across the goalkeeper and low into the opposite corner.

I can run that through my mind like a film, every step of it. I'd never seen a goal to touch it, and I knew I never would again unless he scored it; jammed in at the Kop end with all the others, all of us shouting the "Joey-Joey-Joey!" chant, then falling down the terraces like an avalanche, which could have been frightening. But it wasn't, it was marvellous; people were laughing, not screaming. Right out of control, we were, it was like being carried by a great big wave, you didn't know when the hell you'd stop and yet you didn't care, you were only sorry when you did stop.

Five days I stayed in my room. I didn't shave, I hardly ate. Reporters came; television, and all, but I wouldn't see them. I told my mother, send them away, they're like vultures.

Ted came round, my married brother. He said, "You weren't to blame, John, everyone's agreed on it. He ran out, there was no way you could stop yourself in time. As if *you'd* purposely have done a thing like that. You'd be the very last."

I said, "Everyone?" I said, "How the hell do *they* know? If I'd not been there, it would never have happened. And that's all that counts."

The one person I thought about at all, other than *him*, was Louise. Not at first. I was too numb at first with all the shock of it. Just dead to everything. Then when I did start thinking about her I thought, she's sure to finish with me, now, with how she'd felt about Joey: it'll be the end of *that*, as well. And I accepted it; how else could it be when he'd been so big in both our lives, Joey, when she went on him as much as I did, more in a way, with her being a girl, and girls all liking him so much. She'd as many pictures of him stuck up on her wall at home as I had, including the lifesize, and others of him on the beach, on holiday in Italy.

She'd been with me on Saturday, on the terraces; she'd been with me that day against the Arsenal, too, we'd been swept right down together, holding on to one another, laughing.

Then she did come. My mother said, "It's Louise; will you see her?" And first I had this sort of shock – *she's here, Louise!* – bringing me back to life, then I went numb again, then in the end I said, "Okay, I'll see her."

She came in and at first she just stood there. She was wearing her blue and white City scarf, like she always did. She said, "I'd have been before. Your mother said you didn't want to see anyone."

I was sitting in a chair, I didn't get up, I was looking down at the floor. She said, "It wasn't *your* fault, John."

"I know," I said, "they've told me that."

She said, "As if you'd do a thing like that; of all people, you," and I said, "I'd have cut my leg off, I'd have changed places with him, honest."

She said, "I know you would, John," and she took my hand, which set me off crying, again. Yet at the same time I was wondering how could I ever marry her now when she'd always bring it back to me, more than anybody else.

The doctor came once or twice. He gave me pills to take, tranquillisers, and a letter to the bank so I wouldn't have to go back. Then there was another copper came; he wasn't bad, he stood there in the middle of the room in his big policeman's boots, asking me questions about the accident, taking things down in his book. He told me there was going to be an inquest, and when I heard that I could have died, I really wanted to die. Having to go through it all again, the whole thing again, and in public, with people looking at me. What were they going to say, what would they do to me, because he was God here, was Joey.

Did you find people blamed you?

Some did, yes, some blamed me; but no worse than I blamed myself. They couldn't do.

In court there was his father and mother; that was the worst of it. They'd come down from Scotland and they sat there in the courtroom, looking at me, you did it, you killed him, it was you run over Joey. Every time I met their eyes, it was like being stabbed. I wanted to explain, I wanted to come down from that witness-box and tell them, that I'd *loved* Joey, that I'd worshipped

Joey, that I'd do anything, literally, to make him come alive again... that I wished it had been me instead of him. Only I could tell that they just wouldn't listen. Even when the verdict was given, death by misadventure, they kept on looking at me just the same; I couldn't blame them. After all, I'd killed him, hadn't I? Whatever the coroner said, whether I'd done it on purpose or I hadn't.

I wrote to them after, trying to explain things, but I never got any answer. They'd even had this lawyer to question me. What speed was I doing and when exactly had I seen him and why was I so slow in putting on the brakes? Ridiculous questions that couldn't possibly do any good; trying to catch me, playing games with me. What's the point of it? I kept on thinking, what's the use? As if all this can bring him back again. If they could only do that, they could jail me for life, I'd go willingly. They could even hang me if they wanted.

And *my* parents, on the other side of the court from what they were, looking at them now and then, but them never looking back. They tried to talk to them once, outside the court, but apparently those two, they just turned their backs and walked off. "As if you were a criminal," my mother said, "as if you'd for a minute meant it."

The plans I made then, when it was all going on. To emigrate; to start a new life in Australia, or maybe Canada. To join the Merchant Navy. To change my name, and go to London. I wouldn't go back to the bank, not until after the inquest, and even then I wasn't sure if I would.

That first morning, when I did go back, I remember coming in, not looking left or right, feeling them watching me, all of them; everything dead silent. I went through behind the counter, hung up my coat in the cloakroom there, went over and stood at my old window, and Ron Baker, that was beside me, said, "Are you all right, then, John?" and I said, "Ay, I'm all right."

The whole of that day they never once mentioned what had happened, any of them. It would have been better in a way if they had, because saying nothing made it worse, it hung there in the air, glances, whispering. There were the customers, too, I'd been dreading them the most of all, having to face them, one after another; when I counted the notes, my hands were shaking. A few of them said: "Glad to see you back," but most of them just looked at me like I was a freak, something you pay to see in a circus, a bit frightened, as if they were afraid I might harm them.

I walked out at lunch and I went home. I told my mother that I'd never go back, I couldn't face it, but they were quite good about it; they found me a clerical job away from the counter and I stayed in the end, but it was terrible, still. I felt as though I'd lost a skin. Those days, I don't know how I got through them. It was like the bottom had dropped out of my life, the centre of it.

Before, well, everything really had been City. The morning papers and the evening papers. Who they were going to play that week, who was in and who was dropped, who was fit and who was hurt, who they were trying to buy and who they'd sell, the Football Green on a Saturday night, the match reports on the Sunday morning, Match of the Day on telly on the Saturday night, especially if it was City on. The away games, travelling all over the country, up to Newcastle and down to London, or even abroad, flying, if they were playing in Europe. We'd been as far as Naples once, Louise and me.

Now I couldn't bear to hear their name even mentioned, the City, and as for his name, it was like a knife in me. But wherever I went I'd think I heard it; in the street, on buses, in the cafes. Or see it, catching sight of people's newspapers, even though nine times out of ten I'd be wrong. I'd look closer and see it was some other name.

Then there was the Supporters Club. Before, we'd meet every week, our branch, every Friday night; I was the assistant secretary. I sent them a letter saying I resigned, and three of them came round and called, two of them and Louise. They told me the same old thing, it wasn't my fault, they knew it was an accident, they said, "We know you're just as upset by it as what we are." But I told them no, I'd never come back, I wanted to put it all behind me, forget there was ever such a thing as City. They looked at me like they couldn't believe it. Another thing was I admit I was scared, I was afraid I'd be attacked. In the street, I was forever hearing footsteps behind, especially if I was out at night. I thought that if I ever went near the stadium they'd get me for certain. But I still felt like I was paralysed, which was why I didn't leave, didn't change my job, didn't emigrate, didn't go to London, didn't do any of the things I'd thought about. The centre wasn't there any more, and because it wasn't there, I couldn't act, I just couldn't move.

One night, when Louise came round and my mother and father were both out I went to bed with her and I couldn't do anything, the first time it had ever happened to me. In the end I lost control of myself, I started shouting at her, "Get out, go home, I don't ever want to see you again." I don't know what happened to me.

Except that she was so much part of it.

Mr Gray, I believe it's a year since you were involved in that tragic accident.

A year since the death of Joey Black, yes.

And today, before the kick-off at the City ground, you placed a wreath on the centre spot in his memory.

That's correct, yes.

How did it feel?

It was the proudest moment of my life.

The proudest I've ever known, the proudest I ever *will* know. Sixty thousand of them, all of them cheering me as I walked out there with the flowers, cheering me, and through me, cheering *him*. What they were saying was that they'd forgiven me. It was so different from the first time I'd gone back after it had happened.

After three months. Only through Louise telling and telling me: "You've got to go, you must go," and me turning her down, because every time I even thought about it it would make me feel sick, even the idea of the place. The floodlight pylons, which were always the first thing that you'd see when you drove up the Lancaster Road, thrusting up over the roofs, then the rosette sellers and the newspaper placards and inside, inside the ground itself, the pitch; maybe green at the beginning of the season, rich and smooth, then thick and muddy, in the winter, then, by the spring, all patchy, brown, most of it, just fringed with green along the touchlines. And him not there; them coming out of the tunnel without him, the cheer sounding different, I *knew* it would sound different. The disappointment, the crowd half hoping he'd be there again, a miracle would happen and he'd trot out with them, that long hair bobbing up and down, knees coming up high, the way they did when he ran on to the field. Nine, ten, eleven and not one of them him, with me there knowing it was my fault that he wasn't.

I wore a balaclava helmet that day, the only time I've worn one in my life; a balaclava helmet and on top of that a trilby hat with the brim pulled down, like a gangster. We didn't stand the Kop end, either, like we always used to, in among all the regulars, I couldn't bring myself to face them yet; we stood the other end, behind the Crawford Road goal. I was frightened to death I'd be recognised, that they'd go for me, because there'd been all these phone calls and letters, some of the things they said you'd not believe, the filth that can pour out of people. Three in the morning the phone rang once; I went downstairs and there was this voice, "John Gray?" I said, "Yes, what is it?" and it said, "We'll kill you, you bastard, we're coming round to get you," and others, too, and all those terrible letters. I thought to myself then, if they only knew; because what could they do worse to me than what I was doing to myself? The end of it was we had to change our phone number.

They did bad at first, City, after Joey died, lost the next three on the trot. I tried not to find out what was happening but you couldn't avoid it. The thing seemed to weigh on the whole city, it was like a fog, everyone seemed to be living in mourning. You could tell it from the way they walked, their faces, the tone of their voice. People seemed to talk low, they mumbled, and I know I wasn't just imagining it, it wasn't only me. In fact when you're as low as what I was, you notice things a lot more, you're sensitive to things.

I didn't go to his funeral because they had it in Scotland, but I went to the memorial service they had here a few weeks after; on my own, right at the back. There was hundreds there in the Cathedral, a lot of them crying, and when it came to the part about men growing up and being cut down I went cold, I couldn't move, it felt like everybody in the whole Cathedral had turned round and was looking at me; *you* did it, *you* did it, look at him, there he is.

But it passed, and then we sung *Abide With Me*, like at the Cup Final, and suddenly for the first time I begun to feel better, I honestly believe that was the turning-point. Hundreds of us, all singing, all City fans, like we might have sung *You'll Never Walk Alone* on the terraces. We were together in what we felt, in what Joey had been to us.

And the sermon was beautiful, too; it was preached by the Dean, a tall old fellow with a big, hooked nose and a ring of white hair, he talked about them that the gods loved dying young, he said that Joey's life had been perfect in a way, this was how we ought to think of it, because he'd gone out on the crest, we'd always remember him as a shining star of the football field, somebody who'd lived and died a hero.

I came out of that church and I can't tell you how I felt, different than I'd felt for weeks, like something, some great burden, had been lifted, at last I was alive again. There were other things he said that kept coming back to me, how we were all part of a great scheme, every one of us, how none of us could understand it but each one of us had our part in it, and I thought about this a lot, I realised I was in it, too, and gradually it came to me that maybe this was meant to happen, maybe there was a purpose even to this; and day by day, things changed.

I thought about it all, about him, just as much as I ever had, but now it was a different sort of way, the way the old Dean had talked about, not so much mourning for him now as *remembering* him, thinking of him as he *had* been, at his best, scoring goals, flying past tackles, all the things he'd meant and done, when he was still playing.

I rang Louise and met her again, in a cafe because I didn't want to be alone with her yet, but it went quite well, in fact a lot better. She was pleased to see me, I was happy to be with her. A week or so later she did come round and this time everything was right.

One day I put his picture up again; the lifesize one. I'd not destroyed it; it was in a cupboard under the stairs with all the rest of the stuff, the photos and the rosettes and the banners, the blanket that had all the club badges on, 200 of them, the 5,000 programmes. I couldn't bring myself to chuck them all away, especially the photographs of *him*, it would have been like sacrilege, but I couldn't bring myself to look at them, either, so that's where they were, that's where they'd stayed. I waited for Louise to come before I put it up again, the lifesize, I wanted it to be a kind of little ceremony, and she realised this. We put it up together, then we sat on the bed holding hands, looking at it for a while, then we made love.

John, it was you who initiated the Joe Black Memorial Award?
It was, yes.
Was this your way of making amends?
I suppose you could say that.
And what does the award consist of?
It consists of the sum of £50 and a silver statuette of Joe Black, in action, which is presented every year to the young City player who, in the opinion of the Joe Black Memorial Award Committee of the Supporters Club, has shown most promise during that season.

That first match. The feeling when they came out, and no Joey with them, the emptiness. I knew Louise could tell how I felt, because she gripped my hand, but when the game began, the feeling went away.

I watched at first without a sound, which wasn't like me at all. In the old days I'd have joined in all the chants, I'd be yelling my head off. But suddenly they scored, right down our end, whoosh! A lovely shot, the ball bulging the top of the net out right in front of us, and that released it. I shouted, it was like a spell had been broken. From that moment, I was shouting to the very end.

We won 3-1, it was Everton we beat, and I think this showed me something else, that there'd *always* be a City, any road for as long as *we* could see, just as there *had* been one for nearly 90 years; long before Joey, long before me, long before even my old man had ever stood on these same terraces. City went on and life went on and I went on, and as for Joey Black, I realised the important thing now was that people mustn't forget him. That was my duty, now, to see they didn't, to preserve his memory; that was how I could make up for what I'd done.

The very next Supporters Club meeting, I went down there, and told them what I'd thought. They were all of them very nice to me, they asked me: "Why haven't you been before, lad?" They thought it was a wonderful idea and when we announced it there was a lot of publicity, articles in the papers and all. The money came pouring in and we had this beautiful statuette made, Joey running with the ball at his feet, just like him, just about to kick it, taken from a photograph.

The first season I presented it myself to the kid who'd took Joey's place, Colin Brooks; they had the telly cameras there and I don't know how many reporters. I'd been afraid before that I'd not be able to speak, but when the time come I did, it just came pouring out, a tribute to Joey, what he'd been to all of us, how no one had admired him more than me but what we were here for now was to honour his memory and use it as an inspiration to help City and the players that came after him, because that was what Joey himself would want.

Do you still think about the accident at all, John?

Now and again, yes. But you can't go back in life or football, can you? You must go forward.

Footballers don't cry

The phone went at one in the morning, and I knew who it was. Oh, no I thought, not him, but it had to be him. We'd only got the baby off an hour ago. "Peter," he said, "I've lost me job." There were tears in his voice. It was pitiful, honestly. Him. The Iron Man. But I couldn't sound surprised. It had been coming for weeks.

"Called me in tonight and sacked me," he said, "the bastards." This was what shocked me; his tone. The feeling sorry for himself, after all he'd dinned into me over the years, right from the very beginning. Don't squeal. Pick yourself up and get on with it. Footballers don't cry. Football's a game for men, not lasses. If they kick you, you kick 'em back. All that, and so much more. Never give up. Never to feel sorry for yourself. And now here he was, how they'd done this to him, how they'd done that to him, full of self-pity, wanting comfort, till it was almost like I was him now and he was me.

"Peter," he said, "Peter. I hope you'll never know what it's like to have this happen to you. To be stabbed in the back by a lot of ungrateful, fat-arsed businessmen that know fuck all about this game. That's what hurts. To take it from them; me, that's given my life to the game."

I was still half asleep. I said, "Yes, Dad. I know, Dad." Marion came out of the bedroom, yawning and rubbing her eyes: "Who is it?" and I said, "It's Dad. He's just got the push."

"Not again," she said. "It's the middle of the night. You're going to wake John."

"Dad," I said, "I'll phone you in the morning." I felt bad: I knew he wanted to go on, pouring it all out, and I felt worse, because I knew I didn't want to listen. "God bless you, Dad," I said. "I'll phone first thing tomorrow." Then I put down the phone and took it off the hook, else I knew he'd be back. It was a terrible thing, that. Little moments, little movements, yet you're changing a whole life.

I didn't sleep. I lay awake, thinking. What he'd done for me, how much I'd always admired him. Just a little lad, going to watch him play, at Bolton and

133

at Rotherham; then later on, when he dropped out of the League, at Wigan and Boston and Kettering. Get in, Dad! Go on, Dad! A centre half, great big fellow, coming in bang with his thick legs, ploughing through the mud with his sliding tackles, taking the man, the ball, the lot; jumping above the centre forward, thump with his head, always first to the ball, a hard man, very tough, very brave, very strong, a bit dirty; though I never thought that, then.

All those little back gardens. Left foot, right foot, left foot. "Come on, Peter, come on!" I was frightened of him, me. Him so big and me so little. Like Mother; never really growing.

"You'll be a winger," he said, when what I wanted was to be a centre half, like him. Big and strong. Coming in like a tank.

Later, there were all the piddling little jobs he had, coach of this, manager of that, of nothing. Clubs in the Midland League, clubs in the Northern Premier, always in debt, playing in front of a few hundred people; him having to do everything, mark out the pitch, mow the grass, treat the injuries. "Peter," he'd say, "you're my answer, son. When you make it, I'll make it. The war did me, Peter, as a player. Took the best years of my career away. Stopped me realising my potential. If I'd played for England like I should, there'd have been no stopping me afterwards. Manager of Arsenal, manager of Everton. Look at Matt Busby. Captain of Scotland, end of the war – manager of Manchester United. A great team ready waiting for him. Me, I had to start with rubbish. I've done miracles with rubbish. Worked wonders with rubbish. I knew about recycling before it had ever been invented. But you get no medals for that."

And he hadn't. He'd last three months here, six months there, then something would snap, he'd quarrel with the chairman, blow his top to the Press, even thump one of the players, and out he'd go, off we'd go; another little house, poor Mother packing and unpacking all over again. No wonder she was worn out. No wonder she died.

"But you, Peter," he'd say, "you will justify me. By your career. By your skill. By your determination. And then, Peter, they may begin to listen. They will begin to see that I practise what I preach; through my own son, who nobody can say I did not develop. He'd put his hand on my shoulder, this very emotional look in his eye. "You'll never disappoint me, Peter: I know that."

I wouldn't; I knew it too. I'd rather cut my leg off.

I'd never been so chuffed as when he got the job with City. More than when I came to Rovers, and to London. Even more than when I first played for England. And, to be honest, I think I know why. There was relief in it.

Not just because he'd be happy now, he'd stop complaining now; but because, in a funny sort of way, things were like they should be again. Me an England player, but him a top manager. With only one thing spoiling it; for him, not me. Knowing people were whispering and hinting. Would he have ever managed City if he hadn't been my father, if I wasn't playing for England? Ignorance, that was.

"And why did I play for England?" I'd ask, whenever I got wind of it. "Because of him; Dad and his coaching." But you could see by their faces that you'd not convinced them.

I couldn't even convince Marion. "He didn't make you," she said. "I'm sick of hearing that; from him and you. He was lucky to have you."

"No, no," I said, "you don't know football, Marion."

"I know him," she said, "and I know you."

The next morning, when we woke, the first thing she said was, "He's not coming to stay, is he?" "I don't know," I said. "I've not thought."

She'd never forgiven him, though I've always told her it was nothing personal, nothing against her, even if he was wrong; just his feelings for me, and my football.

"You mean him and your football," she'd said.

He'd always told me, "Don't get married early." I'd tried to explain it to Marion. "It's not you," I said.

"No," she'd said, "and it's not you either; it's him, everything for him. He wants you to be a little puppet, dancing to his strings."

It was a bad time for me, that, pulled one way and then the other. My form suffered. I loved her, I loved him; and I loved football. That was the time I missed a penalty in the semi-final against Leeds at Villa Park, and we went out of the Cup. I didn't see her for a week and I wouldn't talk to him. Then one day I walked into the hairdresser's where she worked and said, "Come on, I've got the licence," because it had to be like that; I either had to marry her or give her up, and if I gave her up it would shatter me.

"My mother," she said, "my father..." but I told her, "Never mind them, and never mind my father. I've got two witnesses; we'll have the church wedding later"; and we did. I'd had to do it like that. For the first time in my life, I'd started hating him.

"My own son," he's said since, "and I wasn't invited to his wedding."

When we stepped out of that gloomy little registry office, I went straight into the post office along the road and I sent him a telegram: MARION AND I MARRIED TODAY BIGGEST MATCH OF ALL LOVE

PETER. We didn't hear from him for ten days, and then he sent a silver teapot that must have cost him a bomb.

"Marion," he said, when he came over from Hartlepool, where he was coach then, "I want you to know I've got nothing against you. I never have had; I've always thought you're a wonderful girl, but Peter and me, we've always lived for football, and I'll admit I've been anxious for his career."

"No more than what I am, Mr Coleman," she said.

But things changed; it was inevitable. The moment we walked into that registry office, they'd changed; it was the first big thing in my life I'd ever done without him, the first I'd ever done against him. But when he got the City job, that changed things, too; it helped to change them back again. It wasn't me getting two hundred quid a week while he got forty any more, and much too proud to accept anything. Time and again I'd say, "Look, Dad, it's yours, you did it; I'd be nothing without you." "I'll not take a penny," he'd say. "The satisfaction I've had from you, you can't buy it." He's a wonderful man, if you only but know him.

So after breakfast, while Marion was feeding the baby, I telephoned him. He was still in the same state. "They're being very vindictive about it," he said. "There's still nearly eighteen months of my contract to run. Ten grand they owe me, and they've as good as told me I can sue them for it. And this club house; they're turning me out of that, as well."

"Dad," I said. What else could I say? "Come down and stay with us."

"You're sure?" he said. "How about Marion? What about the baby?"

"There's tons of room, Dad," I said. "Marion won't mind. Just until you get settled. Till you get another job."

"For a week, then," he said. "But only that, mind. Just till I get fixed up."

She was choked when I told her, Marion. "Without even asking me," she said. "Just for a week," I told her, "while he looks around. He's shattered, Marion."

"He'll shatter us," she said.

He was in a state when he got to us. All tense and taut, that twitch at the left side of his mouth. "It'll be down to your knees, soon," he said, looking at my hair. His was the short-back-and-sides he'd always had. "Hello, Marion," he said. He kissed her on the cheek, and she took it like it was a vaccination. Then he kissed John, the baby, and his face relaxed; he liked the baby. He started playing with his fingers, but he burst out crying.

"He's tired," Marion said, and took him away.

The old man glanced around the place. It was a lovely house; it had cost thirty thousand. Nice, big rooms, big picture windows, looking out on a golf course at the back, colour telly.

"By gum," he said, like he always did, "things have changed a bit since I were playing." I hoped he wasn't going to come out with the usual rigmarole, my hair, my hundred-pound suits, my embroidered shirts, because I knew it by heart: "What's that? The Playboy Club? In my day it was eight pound a week and a pint at the boozer."

Now he looked out the front and said, "That your new car?" It was an XJ Jag. He shook his head; I was used to that as well. "I don't know," he said. I hoped he wouldn't go on about buses and bicycles.

He sat down on the leather sofa, he slapped himself on the knees, he gave the laugh he always gives when he's miserable, and he said, "Well! Now let's wait for the offers to come pouring in!"

"It's early days, Dad," I said. "Oh, yes," he said, "I don't expect them to come rushing. Not falling over themselves. After all, where did I leave City? Only three places off the bloody bottom. Where will they finish now I've gone? Right at the bottom."

"Don't feel bitter, Dad," I told him.

"Bitter?" he said. "I'm not bitter. I'm resigned to it, me. Directors, bloody amateurs, obstructing a professional."

"That's the system, Dad," I said. "You'll not change it."

"It's a bloody diabolical system," he said, and I was afraid he'd be off on another of his favourite moans – directors and how ignorant they were – but instead he went quiet, not even looking at me, sitting there like he was embarrassed, till at last he said, "You don't think there'd be something for me at Rovers?"

It left me speechless. It was the first time in my life he'd ever asked me for anything. "Well, Dad," I said, "there might be. Not as manager, just now, nor as coach. They go together, do those two; everywhere Geoff Creamer goes, Bobby Birchall goes with him."

"I know," he said, "I didn't mean that," which made it worse, because what else was there? Scouting? Looking after the Reserves? Those weren't for Dad; they never had been.

"Maybe I could help with the coaching and the scouting," he said. "Something like that. Weighing up teams they're going to play." He looked at me. The look was new as well, almost pleading. What had happened to him?

"I'll try tomorrow," I said. "I'll see the boss." Then I made an excuse and left the room. It was too much for me.

I did talk to the boss, Geoff Creamer, next day. He was uneasy, I could tell he didn't want to upset me. At the same time obviously he knew about Dad, his reputation. "There's not much for him here, Peter," he said, "not for him."

"Just a bit of scouting and coaching," I said, "to be going on with. It's shattered him, this. I think maybe he needs to get his confidence back."

"I'll talk to the chairman," he said, and a couple of days later he called me in and told me, "We've got something for your father, on the lines he asked for. I'm afraid we can't pay him a lot, but if he regards it as a port in a storm…"

So he started with them, coaching and scouting like he'd wanted, going to look at teams and players for the boss, taking individual players for special skills, out at Epsom, where we trained, nice and near my home. Of course, I was glad he'd got the job, very glad – for him – but it made things strange. Him being at the club, him living at the house. We'd gone back, and yet, if you see, we hadn't gone back. Dad couldn't change; you couldn't expect him to. He'd still tell me what to do, how to play, when to go to bed, even when to go on the job – "Never the night before a match; it's like losing two pints of blood" – like I was still a kid. Marion could hardly keep quiet if she was there when he did it; she'd wriggle, she'd make faces; I was afraid any moment she'd say something, and afterwards she would.

"I don't know how you put up with it. Treating you like a baby, and he wouldn't have a job if it wasn't for you."

"I know," I said. "That's why I put up with it. He knows it, too. He's on forty-five a week; our reserves earn more than that, but without him what would I be earning?" But it wasn't easy to get her to see it like that, especially with the baby, keeping her up and taking all her time. She said, "I've heard of mothers-in-law…"

Once a day he'd say, "I must move out. I mustn't burden you. I'll find a room in a hotel."

"If I hear that once more," Marion told me, "I'll go straight out and find one for him."

I took her hand; she looked very tired. "I know," I said. "I know."

But I couldn't hurt him, even if it sometimes drove me up the wall, the diagrams, the salt and pepper pots on the table, the "action replays", as I thought of them, going over and over some move I'd made or hadn't made, like after a game we lost at home to Newcastle.

"The one-two," he said. "It was on. It was screaming at you. Even with that big camel of a centre forward of yours. Going through alone: that was daft, but then you always were a greedy little bugger."

Another time I missed a penalty at Birmingham. That was good for a week, that. My run-up. The way I'd struck the ball. Hitting it high instead of keeping it low. The position of my body. The goalkeeper's position. "Low and angled, low and angled. How many times do I have to tell you that?"

A million.

Mind, it was only a year ago or so I'd stopped the phone calls, or most of them, the post-mortems we'd have after every big game, even in Europe, especially with England; I remember phoning him once from Caracas, when I really felt I'd played bad. It began to fall off after I got married. Marion would say, "Phoning your father again?" or "I suppose you'll be on the phone for an hour tonight." Perhaps I'd outgrown it, I didn't need it so much now, but she could never realise how it had helped me all those years.

Now and again I'd look at his face when he thought I wasn't and I'd see the bitterness, the disappointment. That was the end, with City – I knew it and he knew it – the end as far as managing a big club was concerned. He'd upset too many people. No wonder he was afraid to leave us, no wonder he was for ever lecturing me; I was all he'd got left.

And then it started at the club. I'd been afraid it would. First he didn't reckon the coach, Bobby Birchall, which was par for the course; he never reckoned any coach, especially one that was coaching me. He'd be out on the field there at Epsom when Bobby was working with us, shaking his head, clicking his tongue, making faces, till it was obvious that Bobby noticed and naturally he didn't like it. There was no future in it either. It was like I'd told him; where Geoff Creamer went, Bobby Birchall went. Geoff Creamer sat in the stadium and handled the directors and the Press, Bobby Birchall was out at Epsom looking after the tactics and the training. If you knocked Bobby, you were getting at Geoff.

One day Geoff had me into the office; he said, "Peter, you'll have to talk to your father." I'd been expecting this. "We're glad to have him here," he said, "till he gets something else, but he must realise Bobby Birchall is coach; and I'm the manager."

"I know," I said, "but it's difficult for Dad. He's used to helping me."

"Just a quiet word," the boss said. "I shouldn't like anything to go wrong," and he gave me what we used to call his Man Management smile, the smile on the face of the tiger. Of course, I didn't talk to Dad; how could I? He'd no time for Bobby, and even less for the boss. "They'll burn you out, this club," he'd say, "using you like they do. This 4-4-2. They want you on both bloody wings; and fetching and carrying in midfield. I'm going to have a word with Geoff Creamer, if it goes on. You'll not last three seasons. I'll tell him, 'You're killing the goose that lays the golden eggs.'"

"Please don't, Dad," I said. "I can tell him myself."

"Ay," he said, "but you haven't, have you? It's just as well I'm here."

The trouble was there was truth in what he said, like there nearly always was; they had been working me hard, for a couple of seasons now, and I was beginning to feel it, but it wasn't any good telling them; it would just make it worse. I'd wince, sometimes, when the boss and the old man were together.

"Work rate?" the old man would say. "What's all this bloody work rate? Footballers aren't factory hands. Footballers aren't navvies."

And the boss would cock his little head and stick out his little fat arse in the way he had and smile his smile and say, "Football's changed a lot, you know, Ted."

"Maybe," said Dad, "but it hasn't changed for the bloody better."

The big blow-up came when we played Milan in the first leg of the European Cup-Winners' Cup quarter-final, at our place. Everything went wrong in the first half. They were playing this packed defence with a sweeper, body-checking a lot, shirt-pulling, and when they broke away and scored we got desperate, just banging long balls into the middle, which their defence were eating.

At half-time, Bobby and the boss came into the dressing-room with the old man, who'd been sitting on the bench with Bobby – they'd sent him out there to watch Milan. As soon as I saw him I could tell we were in for trouble; I knew that look on his face. He was bursting to bollock everybody in sight and, to make matters worse, the boss and Bobby just stood there like a couple of dummies with nothing to offer at all. I was longing for them to say something, anything, just to fill the silence, before the old man leapt in; which he did.

He started, "Well, if you two haven't got anything to say, I have. I've never seen such a pathetic exhibition. You're playing right into their hands. No skill, no method, no intelligence." On and on he went, and whether the other two were too surprised to try and stop him or too chicken I don't know. The fact is they didn't. He bollocked us for using long balls into the middle; he bollocked us, especially me, for not going to the line and pulling the ball back – "You try getting there," I said, "with the shirt-pulling and the obstruction" – and he was still at full blast when the buzzer went for the second half. Bobby and the boss hadn't opened their mouths; we left the three of them behind us in the dressing-room, and I wondered what they'd say to one another.

The thing was that his pep talk worked; I think that's what they couldn't forgive him. We did get our tails up; we did start playing better; we did start going round the back of them; we equalised, and very nearly won.

After the match the boss didn't show in the dressing-room at all, just Bobby, looking a bit sheepish, and the old man, who of course was just full of it; he never could read situations outside football. "That was better, lads, that was better. If you'd played like it the whole of the game, you'd have bloody annihilated them!"

But all I kept wondering was where the boss was, and what he was saying to the chairman. There was a reception afterwards, the usual drag, speeches, a cold buffet, and a couple of beers at most, because you knew the boss was looking. He didn't speak to the old man, nor did any of the directors. There was what you might call an atmosphere.

The word went round that a few of the lads were going on to the Sportsman's Club. I asked Dad if he'd like to come, nearly got my head bit off. "A club? After a game like this? If you'd been trying, you'd all be too tired to do anything but go to bed, which is what you should do, after a match" – another of his favourite moans. So it was a confrontation, the last thing I wanted; the two of us standing there, glaring at each other,

I couldn't back down, not in front of the lads. "Well, I'm going, Dad," I said, "I'll see you later." We went on staring for a while and then he said, "You little tyke," and walked away. I felt bad leaving him.

We were there till nearly three in the morning, but when I got home the light was still on in the front room. He was sitting there with his head in his hands. I'd never seen him look that shattered, eyes all red; he looked a hundred years old.

"They've sacked me, Peter," he said, and he began to cry.

"I'm sorry, Dad," I said and he said, "Sorry? Is that all you can say? You're not going to stay there, are you? You'll ask for a transfer?" But I shook my head.

Get up, I thought, get up; footballers don't cry. The words sprang into my throat and choked me. I knew he'd never get up now.

Everything laid on

I'd noticed him hanging around in the car park, and maybe spoken to him once or twice, but there's dozens of them that come up and like to be seen having a word with you when you've got a bit of fat on it. It makes me laugh now, sometimes, when I go up there to watch a midweek match. People that used to come falling all over you when you were playing for England don't hardly give you the time of day, now you're in the Southern League.

One day before a match this bloke come up to me and says, "Mr. Barker," and I says to him, "Yes, sir, what can I do for you?" I was on top of the world then; international player, club number one in the League; the only thing I never thought about was how long it could last. If I'd known what I know now, they could have kept the Cup, the League and all the lot, and I'd have taken cash for it; only when you're a kid, see, these things mean something to you.

Anyway, this bloke: The first thing you noticed about him was he looked as if he hadn't eaten for a fortnight; cheeks all caved in and hollow like this, long spindly arms and legs, and the dirtiest raincoat I ever seen on anybody. "Mr. Barker," he said, "Charlie" – we was getting familiar – "I wonder if you and one or two of the boys would do me the honour of being my guests tonight at the Apex Club?" Naturally I thought he must be cracked: you could see he wasn't joking with a face like that; I don't think I ever seen him smile, not even when he'd put away half-a-dozen whiskies. You could tell straight off there was something funny about him, he looked like a sort of drawn-out Crippen, with his glasses and his bushy moustache and an old grey hat that stood up straight on his head, what he never took off except when he had to.

So I said to him, "I'm terribly sorry, sir, but me and my pals has already been invited to a coming out ball at the old Savoy, this evening."

"No, Charlie," he said, "I'm serious. If you want to come I've got it all laid on, and you can bring three or four of the others." I started to think a bit at that – after all I didn't want to turn him down, then find out he'd been dead serious the whole time; though another thing was that looking at the way he was dressed, you wouldn't have thought he could afford two dress circle at the Gaumont, leave alone a night club. But you never knew; you'd be amazed if I told you what some of these fans will do, just to get seen with the players.

So when I got into the dressing-room, I told Don Wilkins, Joe Bailey and Jack Clarke – none of them hadn't got married then – what was up, and we agreed we'd look out for him afterwards in the car park. Well, there he was waiting for us all right when we come out after the game.

"Congratulations, Charlie," he says, "congratulations, Don, a wonderful game, wonderful win."

"All right, me old cock," I says, "the lads and me are on. Where do we meet?"

"You tell me where you want to be picked up," he says, "and I'll arrange it." No kidding. I told him, "You'll be using up a bit of petrol and all. Two of us lives near here, but the other two are round Woodford, and Canning Town way."

"It doesn't matter," he says. But the end of it all was we all decided to go home and get smartened up and meet him in a pub near Leicester Square.

Even when I got there and saw the others, I still couldn't believe it was going to come off; it seemed too good to be true. But the bloke turned up all right, like he said he would, and outside he'd got the biggest bloody Rolls-Bentley I ever seen in my life; as big as a team coach. There was room for the whole United side in there, and a couple of reserves to travel. Chauffeur driven, too. All the way there I was kidding the old chauffeur, "Here, James, you took that corner a bit smartish, old chap, didn't you?" but in private I couldn't make up me mind how a bloke like him had got hold of a car like that.

Anyhow, the rest of the night went through like clockwork. He'd got a smashing table in the Apex Club, right up in front, and as soon as we arrived he fixed us up with four hostesses. There was as much as you liked to drink and the band was playing sambas and rhumbas and I was going round the floor with this platinum blonde hostess who I'd taken a fancy to, and hoping I wasn't going to wake up.

When the cabaret come on, Lenny Harris – that was his name, he'd told us – leaned across to me and said, did I like the blonde? "You're dead right I do," I said, so then he whispered that if I liked, we could all of us go back together to his flat, he'd be glad to have us. I said I'd be glad to come, so in a few minutes he put it to the others, and they all said yes except for Jack, who wasn't lasting the pace too good.

It was round about two in the morning that we must have left the club, and he drove us back to his flat out near Hyde Park; the chauffeur must have got tired of waiting and gone home. The flat was like Buckingham Palace, I never seen so many rooms. Carpets as thick as Wembley and cushions you sunk in so deep you thought you'd never come up again.

I was sitting on a sofa with my little bit, Don Wilkins and Joe Bailey were across the room with theirs, and Harris had his on his knee, though I could see that he wasn't really interested. Anyway, I'm not kidding, you could do what you liked with them, and by the time they'd gone home and Harris had fixed the three of us up for the night, I was glad there weren't going to be no midweek matches that week.

By the time I got up it was Sunday afternoon and the other two had gone home. Harris was fussing all round me like an old hen, "You're sure you're all right, Charlie, you're sure you wouldn't like me to get you some medicine or something?"

"I'm okay," I said. "The best medicine you can give me is more of what we had last night."

"Any time you like, Charlie," he says. "Just ring me up any time you feel like it, and bring along any of the boys that wants to come."

The next week was just one long party. When we come out of the ground after training he'd have taxis there waiting for us, to take us wherever we liked. We'd go and watch the nude shows in Soho or go to the Windmill in the afternoon, and in the evening we'd go round to his place and have a party. The funny thing was he never looked like he was enjoying himself; in fact like I said, I don't think I ever seen him smile, not once, let alone laugh. He just said, "As long as you and the boys are enjoying yourself, Charlie." I said to him, "You're dead right we're enjoying ourselves. Ah well, life's a bowl of cherries; if they're going to get eaten at all, you gotta eat them while you're young."

All he said to that was, "What do you think's going to happen in the Cup tie on Saturday, Charlie?"

I said, "The way we're all going on right now, none of us are going to be able to get out on that field, never mind play."

That got him worried and he said, "Do you think so, Charlie? Is that really what you think? Maybe I better stop everything until it's over."

"Don't you worry, old son," I said, "you just go right on. We won't have no trouble beating that lot, they're nearly bottom of the Third North."

"Yes," he said, "but Cup ties."

"Don't worry, Lenny," I said, "just leave it to me. What did I tell you; life's a bowl of cherries."

Now and again I tried to find out what he did for a living, but you couldn't ever pin him down. "I'm in business," he said, looking away from you like as if he was ashamed of it.

"Well, what sort of business?" I asked him. "Because if you've got room for a junior partner, I'm on, I'd hang up me boots tomorrow."

"Oh, no, Charlie," he says, "no, no. Please don't do that."

"If you ask me what Lenny buys and sells," said Don Wilkins, "it must be diamonds." He took it all quite serious; shook his head and said no, it wasn't nothing to do with jewellery. Anyhow, by the time it come round to Thursday, only four or five of us could last the pace.

I used to roll up for training, and some mornings I couldn't hardly put one foot in front of the other, but I'd made up me mind it didn't matter; if the worst came to the worst, I could always drop out. They didn't need me to win at Rochdale.

After a couple of days Lenny started coming out of his shell a bit. He still didn't drink much and he still didn't go with the girls, but what he did was to start giving us advice. "You don't mind my saying this to you, Charlie," he'd say, "but if you ask me, you aren't using the square ball enough."

"Thank you, Mr. Harris," I said, "I've been thinking the very same thing myself: I'm glad you brought it up and reminded me."

But he never had no idea when someone was taking the mickey, he just said, "Anything to help, Charlie; anything to help United."

"You want to put some of them ideas of yours up to the manager," I said, "to Mr. Groves. He'd be grateful for a bit of outside help planning the tactics wouldn't he, Don?"

"I'll ring him up," he said, "when's the best time to get him?" Don Wilkins looked at me and I looked back at him, and it was all we could do to keep ourselves from laughing ourselves sick.

You could get anything you wanted out of him, too. One day I looked at his suit and I said, "That's a nice suit you're wearing, Lenny. I wouldn't half mind having a suit like that."

"Here you are," he said, "I'll give you the name of my tailor. Go round and get yourself measured, tell him to charge it to me." I didn't need no more telling; I was round there the next morning. Don Wilkins got a pair of shoes, Joe Bailey got shirts, and Jack Clarke got half-a-dozen ties. We was walking around like the best dressed team in London. But another funny thing we noticed about Lenny was he didn't never really seem to be at home in the places he took us, like if we wasn't used to all that carry-on, he wasn't used to it either.

"Did you get on to old Grovesy about them square balls?" I asked him and he said, "I tried to get through, Charlie, but he wouldn't speak to me. Maybe you could put in a word for me."

"You should of told him who you was, Lenny boy," I says.

When the weekend come round, he told us he was coming up North to see the Cup tie. The team was staying in Manchester and going on by coach to Rochdale in the morning, and Lenny told us he's booked himself in our hotel.

"Lay it all on, Lenny," I said, "bring on them dancing girls. Plenty of champagne, eh?"

"Do you think you really ought to, Charlie?" he says, "the night before the match." "Of course I ought," I says, "there's nothing like champagne to get you really going. All the big French teams train on it all the time, it's so cheap out there. Didn't no one ever tell you that?" "Well, I'll do my best, Charlie," he says.

He came up on the same train as us, and we got him in with the rest of the party. Our club has so many hangers-on when it travels that one more don't make no difference. I even introduce him to Billy Groves, and blow me if he doesn't get on to him straight off about why don't the team use more square balls. Billy's eyes was popping out of his head, but I made a face at him over Lenny's shoulder to tell him that the poor bloke didn't mean no harm.

Most of the lads knew Manchester all right from having played there so often, and our plan was to sneak out of the hotel after dinner to a club where a lot of the local footballers go, where there's always a lot of good crumpet there, and ask some of the girls to come back for a party. Because we had to be back before ten, see.

Well, it all worked out like we wanted, the girls come round, Lenny had the champagne, and we was up there in his room, half-a-dozen of us, until about three o'clock in the morning. Then the door suddenly opens and in come Bert George, the trainer; you couldn't hardly see who it was at first, the cigarette smoke was so thick. He'd come down the corridor for a leak and heard a noise. "All right," he says, "get back to your rooms the lot of you. We'll see about this in the morning."

Lenny springs out of his chair and starts trying to explain, but Bert doesn't even listen to him, he just walks out of the room as if Lenny isn't there.

What happened to us the next day is history. With the run of the ball Rochdale had, they might of beaten us even if we was all fit, but the way some of us was feeling, we didn't have no chance from the beginning. I hit the bar in the first five minutes, but after that I just didn't feel like playing. My head felt like it was coming to pieces and my mouth was so dry I thought I was going to die of thirst. At half time we was a goal down, and in the dressing-room Billy just looks at us and says, "I know what's wrong with you miserable lot all right, and if you don't go out and win this half, God help you." But Rochdale got another goal, and we was out of the Cup.

When we came out of the ground, Lenny was waiting for us, and he'd been crying. There wasn't no doubt about it, you could see the tears all running down his hollow cheeks. He come up to me as if he wanted to say something, but as soon as he saw him Billy said, "Get out of my sight before I kick your arse off. If I ever set eyes on you at our ground again, I'll throw you out myself." Lenny didn't say nothing to that; he just stood there looking at us and crying.

There weren't no taxis waiting outside our ground that Monday. I'd just been suspended for two weeks, but I didn't mind that; the lads always whip round for you and you end up with more than what you'd have in the ordinary way, because you don't pay no tax on it. I went to a phone box and rung up Lenny, but I didn't get no reply. I tried again three times that day, but it was still no go.

"He must be lying low," Don Wilkins says, next morning: he'd tried as well. Then, when we bought the evening paper, there he was – picture on the front page; Leonard Harris, charged with embezzlement. He worked in the Borough Treasurer's office at a county council and he'd fiddled himself eight thousand quid. The funniest thing of all was they hadn't even caught up with him; he'd, given himself up on the Monday morning.

So that was it; we was out of the Cup, and I never got me suit. I know one thing, though; if it had been me had got hold of eight thousand quid, I certainly wouldn't of spent it on no football team.

The dying footballer

"That's right! he said, in a loud, brash Geordie voice. "That's right! A big fellow with a bullet head! I heard you! I heard you in the cinema!"

Sitting there, he seemed to rise out of the bed as sudden and irrelevant as a Triton; the rough, grey jersey, the square, red, wind-whipped face, belonged not to a sanatorium but to ships, fields, stadiums.

"I didn't know…" I said, and stopped, the attack too strong and unexpected. I had probably made the remark, but then I had never seen him, had only heard about him, and the image I had formed was precisely that: a big fellow with a bullet head. Looking at him now, I could see that he was big indeed, but that the head was uncompromisingly square. In the bed beside him, Williams, a small, grey headed Welshman, smiled a secret and diverted smile, and reached for the sputum mug on his pedestal.

"I was right in front of you," Marshall said. "Now then!" His expression was one of challenge, as though he dared me to deny it, his voice the same brass monotone, and it was several moments before I realised that he was not annoyed, that this vehemence might simply be his way of statement. But embarrassment had paralysed me; I mumbled quickly the message I'd been given for them, and I left the room.

A few days later, I had cause to visit them again, this time with a trolley of library books. All those patients who were out of bed had jobs to do, and this was one of mine. Their room was at the very end of the long, dim, ground-floor corridor and when I reached it, I hesitated before knocking on the door.

"Come in!" The voice was not that of a sick man; again I wondered what had brought Marshall here. "What, fetched us some books?" he asked, without reproach. "Let's see 'em, let's have a look at what you've got."

"Here you are, then," I said, annoyed that he should take it for granted.

"Daphne Du Maurier? That's no bloody good to me! Haven't you got nothing new? Something by Micky Spillane? Something with a bit of meat in it?"

"No."

"Then I'll get 'em from home," he said, "I will," and leaned back against his throne of pillows. I had planned to talk to him about his club – the one he managed, and the others he had played for – but at this I muttered, "All right, then," and wheeled the trolley from the room.

"Here, come back!" he called, "come back!" but I took no notice. A week later Dr Cowley said to me, his lean, brown face alive with a joke he would not share, his smile private and condescending, "You can talk about football all day long, now. Mutual therapy. I'm moving you in with a professional."

"Billy Marshall?" I said. "But can't I stay in this room?"

"We need it," he said. "There's a much more serious case than you coming. We're only keeping you because we want to teach you some discipline, anyway."

"But isn't there someone else? "

"*No* one else," he said, his anger rising quickly, as it always did when he was opposed. He was at the door now, disdaining to look at me. "No one else. If you don't want *that* bed, you can go home."

The next afternoon, I moved in with Billy Marshall.

"Hallo, lad," he said. "I'm glad to see you here. I'd rather have you than that other fellow; coughing and spitting all the time, hawking into his cup. It was filthy; filthy."

I nodded morosely at him, and looked out of the window. Beyond the putting lawn, where a group of patients was engaged in desultory play, a rank of pine trees grew like watch towers, their pale, thick bark like the scales of immense crocodiles. Through them, again, one saw the Norfolk fields, pale and unemphatic, gently rising into a grey distance.

"How old are you, lad? " Marshall asked, behind me. "Nineteen? That's a bit bloody young to be in a sanatorium. They tell me you're an Arsenal fan, as well."

"I am," I said, turning round slowly. "You're a bit of fan of something else, too. Eh? I've seen you here, from the window. I've seen you with that girl, that what's it."

"Have you? "

"Ah, and you needn't try that," he cried, with pointing finger, "making out you don't know what I'm on about. I've seen; I'm not bloody blind."

"I'm sure you're not."

I undressed in silence, got into bed, and opened a book, without another word.

"Here, have you seen this?" he said. There was a rustle, something landed on my bed, and, looking up, I saw that a green newspaper, a Football Final, was lying there, irresistible. I thanked him.

"Two goals up," he said, "and let in three in the last twenty minutes. I know 'em. There's no one there to talk to the buggers. They let up, it went to their head."

The paper came from the Yorkshire coast town whose Third Division club he managed. There was a kick by kick match report, spreading over two pages – "Town were moving well now and a sizzling twenty yard drive by star forward Jimmy Wall smashed against United's upright; United's goal was bearing a charmed life" – a honeycomb of local League results, a page of minute, compulsive team analysis.

"You were unlucky to go down last season," I said.

"Unlucky? We weren't unlucky, we were swindled down, it was a bloody scandal. What about the team that stayed up, eh? What about the last match of the season, the one they won away from home, when their centre-half went round the other dressing-room with a bundle of five-pound notes? You can't prove it, you can't get at them, but when I see bloody Stewart, I'll tell him, he'll hear something. I've never had time for that bugger."

"What, the manager of Rovers?"

"If I had my way, he'd be manager of bloody Dartmoor. I've told him so, I've known him twenty years. He's a rogue, that's what he is, a rogue. I knew him when we were both running clubs in the Lancashire Combination; he was with Runcorn, I was player-manager of Rossendale. We went there for a match one day and the gateman said, 'Where's your card? You can't come in without your card, Mr Stewart's orders and I said, 'Bugger Stewart, I'm the manager. You go and tell Stewart I'm here.'

"So he came out and I said to him, 'What's all this about?' and he said, 'You know you're meant to have your registration card, you know it's a League rule,' and I said, 'Bugger that,' and I pushed him in the chest, I pushed him all the way down the bloody corridor."

I could imagine him doing it. The first, giant tactlessness, the sudden gesture, and now this anecdote, revealed him as a force of nature, devoid alike of ruth and malice, so that the common courtesies were not disregarded, but simply unknown. Thus, our days together were pregnant with surprise; my own at sudden monstrous violations of tact, and his surprise at my resentment. Then there would be temporary silences, each of us prisoned in our own astonishment, till the silence would change in quality, from hostility to armistice, and a gesture – usually his – would bring peace again.

He had two visitors during our first week together. One was his wife; she was his own age, a blonde matron-figure, fitting shapelessly into shapeless clothes, all smiles and mild, clucking amazement. Her cheeks were heavy with rouge. She, too, was from the North East, but she had its soft, persuasive accent, where his was vehement and hard; they talked together with a quick, low intimacy. Now and then, there were moments of apparent tension. I could not hear what they said, but she seemed to be pressing him, and his voice would rise, with a note of obstinacy. For all his present illness, I had an impression that she had somehow abdicated from life, while he had not.

There was a son, born late in the marriage, ten years old, but he hadn't come; when Marshall spoke about him it was with a certain reluctant pride, as though he were aware of an Achilles' heel. "Kicks well, he does that; left foot or right."

The second visitor was less expected. She came one afternoon when Marshall was asleep, her auburn head peering round the door a moment, uncertain. Then, opening the door a little farther, she tip-toed into the room, a tall, handsome, large-breasted woman, perhaps in her early thirties. "Billy?" she whispered, and again, a little louder, "Billy?"

His head turned on the pillow, he gave a snort, then sat up very quickly, looking at her. "I'll be buggered. I was asleep."

"I wrote you I was coming." She spoke with a Yorkshire accent. "I know you did, I know." He gestured at me and said, "This is Brian." "The other one's gone, then."

"Well, tell me," he said. "Come on, tell me." He took her hands and she sat down by him, on the bed. I picked up a book and turned my back on them, in deference to their intimacy, but they spoke very little, only a murmur now and then, and once their silence grew so protracted and intense I imagined that they must be kissing. When she'd gone, he did not talk about her, and it was three weeks before she came again. I wondered if his wife knew, and had a notion that she did; at times I'd sensed in her attitude a lurking reproach, and in his an evasive guilt.

It wasn't long before he, too, was allowed to get up and begin the series of graduated walks across the bland, flat country; to the white gate, the stone bridge, the village, and at length, beyond it, to the windmill, the church, the railway station, the sea shore. Marshall would put on corduroy trousers, his jersey, a tweed cap; sometimes he would carry a stick. He walked with a slow, heavy stride, saying, "Go on, lad, go on, I can't keep up with you. I wish I had your wind."

There was something about him that was vaguely obsolete, and at the same time, reminiscent. Later, I identified this feeling with an old, forgotten photograph – of footballers abroad on a Continental tour, between the wars; flat caps, baggy suits off the peg, an impression of stiffness and unease, the Depression invisible in the background. It was from these years that Marshall had emerged, as player, first, then manager, one of the "old school", cut off from the new wave of blue blazers, muted accents, quiet conformity – "If you eat peas with a knife, now, they won't put you in the England team." He'd been born in one of those little Northumberland mining villages where footballers sprouted like dragons' teeth, had turned professional – "Newcastle bloody daft and I signed for Sunderland" – played five times for England, become a player-manager, then a manager.

While we walked, he would talk about all this; of goals, games, players, great victories, unjust defeats. Through his whole narrative ran a thread of rough acceptance; you were hard and football was hard, and football was hard because life was hard. "I had bloody Dougald with me, three year before the war; there was still no one could play like him when he wanted; he could still have played for Scotland, only they'd never have him again after what had gone on, drunk every bloody night. I took a risk, see; I gambled on him. One morning they had a fight in the dressing-room, him and that bloody Irishman, Donnon. Donnon gave him a black eye, and by the time I'd heard of it and went down there, they'd gone, they'd gone to bloody Dougald's house for dinner! I wanted to suspend the two of them, but the Board wouldn't have it, so I took 'em both down to Fulham for the Saturday and Dougald broke his bloody leg."

He wouldn't be in the sanatorium long – he was sure of that, and so was I. "Lie on the bed, do this, do the bloody other. I said to the sister the first day I was here, 'Look, bugger off,' I said, 'you can ask me,' I said, 'you can't bloody well *tell* me, nobody can.' Then *he* comes round the other day, the little one with the big nose, the patients' committee, he says, 'You're up now, you're delivering papers down this corridor.' 'I'm bloody not,' I said, 'not if you put it like that. If you ask me properly I'll do it; willingly. Started off selling papers in Newcastle, I don't mind going back to it now.'"

Even Dr Cowley was wary of him, playing him carefully and respectfully, like some angler who has inadvertently hooked a shark. "All right today, Marshall? Temperature still on-side?"

And Marshall, looking at him, cautious and impassive, "Ay, all right, doctor. Just tell me the day I can go, that's all."

He had a posse of friends, Northerners, like himself, who would emerge from their nooks and crannies – from lofts, from chalets on the hillside – to surround him for a steady grumble, for mutual rough consolation: Jack Grace, with his bald head and his insinuating chuckle, little Dave Oliphant, with his auburn moustache, his bent shoulders and his grinding omniscience; Ernie Jacks, who was sixty, a Yorkshire leprechaun, living in a private and inaccessible world. "The doctors? Booger the doctors!"

"Ay, but you can't bugger them all, Ernie," said Marshall.

"*He* can!" chuckled Grace. "Can't you, Ernie?"

They were all polite to me, but I wasn't one of them, hadn't the common experience, the years, the vernacular, the responses and reactions. I was cautious with them when we were together, glad they seldom joined us on our walks, some because they were still largely bedridden, others because we went too fast and far. "Mad boogers, the pair of 'em," Ernie would say.

Sometimes, as we walked, Marshall would ask, "What am I doing here?" echoing the question that was in my own mind. What, indeed? "Never a day's ill-health; never a day. Two cartilages out and a broken leg; that's the only time I've ever been in hospital."

"Then how did you get *this*?"

"How? I don't know, buggered if I do. I asked the doctor at home; he said, overwork. Overwork? I said. I've worked like this for twenty years. He said, ay, but you're not young any more. Well, I'm not old, I said; I'm not so bloody old."

I could see, at that moment, that in his own eyes he would always be young, and it was this that made his wife seem older than he – this that enabled him to keep the auburn girl, with her big breasts and her nascent sensuality. "I'll be out in a month," he said. "Two months and I'll be running the bloody club again. I told 'em."

In the meantime he went to the clinic once a week, "to get pumped up" – or for his "A.P. refill", as the other patients called it. But Marshall never acquired the sanatorium vocabulary; "thora", "A.Ps.", "P.Ps." "refills", "strep", "P.A.S.". It was as though, by rejecting it, he somehow denied the reality of his illness, his involvement with the rest of us.

The next time his wife came, she brought their son. He was a lively, fair-haired child, with sturdy, plump, pink knees; he climbed on the bed in his excitement while behind him, his mother uselessly exclaimed: "David, don't crawl on him! Get off the bed, will you?"

"He's all right," Marshall said, grabbing the boy and rolling him on his back. She watched them without more protest, almost with resentment, as if she knew that she would always be excluded.

"I were in the school team, Dad! I played and I scored three! "

"You're coming on, you're coming on."

Marshall was beginning, now, to agitate. When Dr Cowley came round in the evenings, he would say, "How about a date, then, doctor? My temperature's still down. I'm gaining weight. I feel well." And Dr Cowley would reply, "Not yet, not yet, it won't be long."

"Ay, but how long? Two weeks? A month?"

"Softly, softly catchee monkey," Dr Cowley said, and disappeared with his crooked, self-conscious smile.

"I'll give him monkey. We'll be up for bloody re-election by the time I get out."

For his team wasn't doing well, in that Northern Section where the names fell like dry ice on the heart; Barrow, Rochdale, Tranmere, Accrington. It was Accrington, indeed, who beat them 6-0, after they had failed to win one of their last four home games. "I wrote to them. I told them they'd get a hiding there, if the wing-halves carried the ball. Both of them go up together, the others break away and they've got the whole park in front of them. And they send missionaries to Africa..."

Autumn turned to winter. It snowed, and the snow dropped slowly from the pines and lay thick upon the hill, with its pink-roofed chalets. The little red flags of the putting lawn rose here and there above the snow carpet like buoys in a white sea. We would spend hours together in the recreation room, playing a game called Disc-Bat Cricket; a game at which I always won.

"Makes his own bloody rules!" he would shout, calling on all present to bear witness. "Two fielders inside the circle; he can do it: you can't!" And sometimes I would lose my temper, shouting back, forgetting that to him a shout meant as little as a shrug, and must never be taken at its face value. The draw for the FA Cup was made; by chance the Rovers, "Bloody Stewart's" club, had been drawn to play nearby, at Norwich. "I'll be there if it does for me," said Marshall. "I'll be there if I go in a bloody ambulance."

The auburn-haired woman came again, and this time, I was able to go out of the room and leave them. An hour later, returning to go back to bed, I found she was still there. Marshall had already got into bed, and she sat there as she had before, her hand in his. "I'll go out," she said, but before she could move there was an eager pattering in the corridor, the door was hurled open, and Marshall's little boy appeared.

"Hallo," said Marshall, looking up. "Clash of fixtures here."

The women, confronted, gave each other one pregnant glance – shock and detestation on the one side, guilt, resentment and a covert defiance on the other, then there was silence. The three of them might have been frozen by a Gorgon's head, with only the little boy bewildered and alive.

"Well," the younger woman said at last, "I'll be going, then." She climbed off the bed, pulled her dress down with a crisp defiance, said flatly, "Get better soon, then, Bill," exchanged tight-lipped goodbyes with Mrs Marshall, and left the room. As the door began to close Marshall found his voice, roaring after her, "Look after yourself, now."

"She's always done that," his wife said, with low intensity, while the little boy cried, "Who's that, Dad? Who's that lady? Why did she go?"

"Just a friend, that's all," he said. "She was passing through. She was going to Norwich." Lying on the next bed, I feigned that I could neither see nor hear, sharing their agony, wondering how long his wife would stay, what they could find to say while she did. But it was the little boy who saved them, busy with his questions, so that Marshall could talk to him while his wife, still sitting there, withdrew, till such time as she could decently leave him. I sensed in her hostile farewell to me that I was included in her indictment, that simply through being there, when she was not, I had somehow conspired to betray her.

"These things happen," Marshall said, when she had gone, "you can't help them," but within half an hour, resignation gave way to good cheer, and he was telling me about Fred Westgarth, the manager of Hartlepools. "He's a rough diamond, Fred, a rough diamond. I rang him up once about fixtures. He said, 'When shall we play?' I said, 'New Year's Day.' He said, 'New Year's Dee? New Year's Dee? When's that?'."

As the day of the Cup-tie approached, he talked increasingly of "Bloody Stewart". "He'll be surprised. He'll never reckon on seeing me there. And I'll tell him in front of the lot of them. I will."

We stood by the mill pond, beneath the silent windmill; three swans floated motionless, haughty and serene. "I'll wake 'em up," said Marshall, "sitting there like they own the place." He beat his stick hard and fast against the boards skirting the pool and at once the three swans turned and made towards him in a menacing glide, quick and effortless, the mean little heads extended at the end of their long, white, powerful necks. "I'll show 'em. Break their bloody necks I will." For the moment, they were Stewart-surrogates.

The first swan hissed and struck, and I backed uneasily away, but Marshall merely stepped aside, and nudged it with the flat of his stick. "I should leave them," I said, "they'll be out of the water." But he took no notice, defiant, just as in past days, he must have defied a packed defence.

"Go on! Get off, you buggers! With a flap of wings, a second swan climbed out of the pond, but again Marshall side-stepped, pushing it away, until the three of them confronted him, hissing and dripping, he motionless, the stick extended. The tableau lasted for perhaps thirty seconds, then all at once dissolved as the swans, one by one, turned and scuttled back into the pond. "There you are," said Marshall, "I told you. Stand up to them. That's all you've got to do." And somehow the whole incident seemed characteristic of him, not only for his defiance, but for the aggression which had made defiance necessary.

At first, Dr Cowley did not want to let him go to Norwich; to deter him he assumed his "ruthless" tone. "If you really want to get pleurisy, you can go, so long as you don't expect me to look after you when you've got it."

"I don't expect anything, doctor; I never have, never in me life."

And so we went, the two of us together, went by taxi, with two tickets for the directors' box. "He'll get a shock," Marshall kept saying, as we sped over the snow-powdered roads, past the dappled fields, past the villages, with their neat Tudor churches. We ate at a Norwich restaurant, full of rowdy, red-faced men, wearing the green and gold favours of the City, shouting in the broad, quick Norfolk accents, "Up the Canaries!" and from time to time bursting into song: "On the ball, the City!

Never mind the *dan*-ger!"

Beyond the ugly railway siding, down the mud track, past the bleak canal, the Stadium was a vacuum pump, sucking the city dry. The air was crisp and very cold, and there was movement everywhere; the fans were bowling along together, side by side, as though to a family occasion.

"I'll give him bloody relegation," Marshall said.

A commissionaire showed us to the boardroom, afume with whisky, beer and cigarette smoke, but the sanatorium had conditioned us, and we sheered away, making for the open air. Beneath the directors' box, the stadium surged with colour and expectancy. The Norwich mascot was a tall, gaunt man with an umbrella, dressed up to look like a canary, with a great artificial beak, a mass of green and yellow "feathers", and a bell which – together with the nose – completed a sinister resemblance to The Bellman, in the Duchess of Malfi.

When Stewart climbed into the directors' box, Marshall greeted him with, "Now then, Tommy!" and Stewart recoiled, as far as his short, plump figure would allow him; a little, round-faced man with silver hair and quick, pale, cunning eyes. "Never thought you'd be here, Billy."

"Ay, I bet you never did!"

"Heard you'd been ill," Stewart said. It was one of those voices which had begun in the North, to be planed and deracinated by years in the South. "Getting better, are you?"

"None the bloody better for seeing you," said Marshall, while the directors' box filled up, each newcomer pausing to observe the cameo, astonished, interested or wary. "Just tell me how you won that last match, eh? Just tell me how you kept out of the Second Division. That's all I've come to ask you." "I don't know what you mean, Billy," Stewart said, looking away from him.

"That last match at Frinton Park. You know." "Fair and square, Bill," said Stewart, "we won it fair and square. I'm surprised at you, complaining."

"Bought it fair and square, you mean!" cried Marshall, while a hubbub of voices rose to drown his own, and Stewart cried, "You be careful, Bill! I can have you into court for that, it's slander!"

"Have me, then!" Marshall shouted. "Have me if you bloody dare! And have your bloody centre-half, as well! The one with the fivers!"

Forgetting, once again, the special nature of his violence, I wondered whether he was going to hit Stewart, and then, what I would do if he did. For he could not be allowed to do anything so self-destructive, so reckless of the sanatorium code of careful preservation. "Billy," I cried, taking his arm, but he paid no notice to me. Stewart was very still and quiet, like some hunted animal which seeks escape through stealth and self-effacement, his eyes turned slyly away. Below the directors' box, spectators were standing up and looking round and indeed, all over the grandstand, clumps of people were rising to their feet, heads were turning curiously towards us. How the scene would have ended I don't know, but it was destroyed in a moment by a sudden, surging roar, a roar taken up all over the stadium – "Up the Canaries!" as the Norwich team, in green and gold, ran on to the field.

"I told the bugger," Marshall said, and sat down, evidently satisfied. At half-time in the board room, people were chary of us, but Marshall was heartily at ease, greeting those he knew, sweeping them into conversation despite themselves. In any case one saw he was a popular man, and apart from Stewart and the Rovers directors, whom he now ignored, they all seemed glad to let their reserve be demolished.

In the taxi, on the way back to the sanatorium, his vitality seemed to leave him. He sat silent, breathing a little heavily, unwontedly withdrawn, as if he were at last coming to terms with the treason of his body. "I wish I had your energy, Brian." Once, he began to cough, and the coughing grew, feeding on itself, raucous and resented, louder and louder, as though he were fighting against each new eruption. He pulled out a large, drab-green handkerchief, bending his head to it, and the bitter, private battle went on, till he relapsed, with an exhausted sigh, in his corner.

"Are you all right now, Billy? "

"I'm all right," he said, in a ghostly wheeze of a voice.

In bed that evening, his temperature had gone up to 100, but he marked it on his chart as 98.4.

"Well, did you both shout yourself hoarse? " asked Dr Cowley. "Did the best team lose?"

"Ay, it did that," said Marshall. "You look a bit pink," said Dr Cowley. "No double whiskies with the directors, afterwards?"

"Never touch it, doctor. Haven't touched it since I've been ill."

"Temperature down?" asked Cowley, taking the chart.

"Same as usual, doctor."

His coughing woke me in the night. I opened my eyes to the dim effulgence of his bedside lamp and saw that for the first time ever, he was using the abominated sputum mug.

"Can I get you a drink of water, Billy?"

"What?" he said, with a quick, covert turn of the head, "you awake, then? No thanks, boy, I'll be all right."

Next day, instead of getting up for lunch, he stayed in bed. His temperature had not gone down; this time, he did not record it at all.

"I told you what would happen," Dr Cowley said, at last in a position of command. "Your temperature's up, you're getting sputum, and I wouldn't be surprised if you've got pleurisy as well." Yet he spoke without recrimination, as though it were sufficient for him to be right.

"Ay, I should have listened to you, doctor," Marshall said, in a slow, reflective voice, and he stared out across the room. "I'd no right to go."

"Perhaps it's taught you a lesson," Dr Cowley said. "You can't play about with this disease, even if you're a footballer. Perhaps you'll take my word for when it's time to let you go home."

"I will that," Marshall said, half-audible.

His friends came to see him in the afternoon; Jack Grace, Dave Oliphant and Ernie Jacks. "What's the matter with you, Billy? Shamming? Don't you want to go home to the wife, then?"

"I got a cough going to Norwich, that's all there is to it. Cough and a bloody temperature." But from the strange lack of emphasis, I knew he feared there was more to it than that. He was still coughing frequently, and whenever he had to use his sputum mug, he would turn his back towards me.

"He's had the last laugh, then, bloody Stewart. If I have got pleurisy, I wouldn't be surprised. I wouldn't. When I cough, I can feel it there."

"Come along to the clinic and we'll have a listen to you," Dr Cowley told him. He was in their hands now, an acquiescent body to be sounded, drained, painfully rehabilitated; no better than the rest of us.

"I *have* got it, then," he said, shuffling back into the room, in dressing gown and slippers. "I can give this season up, the whole of it. They'll have to stay off the bottom without me."

"Oh, they will," I said, "they won't have to be re-elected."

"I wish I was as sure as you are."

He was entirely confined to bed, now, fretting the supine days away, dabbling now in a book, now in a magazine; now putting earphones on, to listen to the radio. He spent two hours one morning in the clinic. "Sticking this in me, sticking bloody that in me," he said, kicking off his slippers with subdued disgust. "They turned me into a bloody dartboard; I thought they'd never be done. Honestly."

The following evening, Dr Cowley came in and said, "Your sputum's positive."

"Thanks," he said. "I'll be here with you for life, then, doctor."

"You might be," Cowley said, with his diabolic grin, and he was out of the door.

In the weeks that followed, Marshall displayed a restless stoicism. It was, as he told his wife when next she came, "me own fault, no one else's. Except Bloody Stewart, maybe, and you can't blame him, really. You can't."

His wife sat with him in melancholy silence, a double reproach now in her eyes. Once, I heard her say, "You shouldn't have gone, Billy. You know you should never have gone."

"Ay, I know, but it's done now. I've learned me lesson." He was eating less, pushing his meals away with a disgust directed at his own lack of appetite as much as at the food itself. "I can't get interested, staying in bed the whole time. It's not natural."

The ritual weighing, which took place each Monday morning in the hall of the sanatorium, now became a ceremony as important to him as to the rest of us. The matron would sit beside the weighing chair, slender and pretty in her white cap and narrow, blue, archaic dress, surrounded as always by an aura of bitter-sweet unfulfilment.

"Well, Mr Marshall, is the centre-forward still carrying too much weight?"

"Too little, matron," he replied, drawing tight the sash of his red silk dressing gown, and grimly climbed into the chair. His face remained set during that silent hiatus in which the weights poised and chinked in her narrow fingers, then at last she said, "You've lost four pounds."

"Wasting away, matron," he said, shaking his head and heavily getting up. "There'll not be any of me left, soon."

Looking at him closely, in our room, I could see his ruddy cheeks had withdrawn a little, yet I could never imagine the face being anything but robust and full.

Later that week, I was moved out of the room, to a chalet on the hillside. It was fresher there and less oppressive, a great step towards ultimate release, and yet I felt I was deserting him.

"You go, lad; good luck," he said, pushing my apologies aside. "Come out soon and join me."

"I'll try, I'll do me best." But now he seemed to speak without optimism.

I visited him every day, and knew that he was grateful; there was a sentimental core to him, however vigorously disguised: it showed obliquely and occasionally. "If you're looking for a film, The Barretts of Wimpole Street; that's the one they ought to show. Everyone would enjoy it. Honestly."

Once, climbing the steps to the sanatorium, I met the auburn-haired woman, coming out. I think she would have liked to glide past, but I stopped her, anxious to show I did not judge her. "What do you think of him?"

She looked away, saying at last, "He's not good, is he?"

"He'll get better quick enough." I was convinced of it.

"I don't know. He's got so thin, like." Seeing him each day, it was something which had not impressed me. "Half a stone he's gone down, since I was here." I could think of nothing to say, and it was she who spoke again, at last. "I brought him a steak. Maybe they'll cook it for him." Then she was off.

After another ten days Marshall, too, was moved from the room; to a single room on the floor above. "I asked him, 'What does it mean? Am I getting worse, then?' But they won't tell you. I said, 'I'm entitled to know,' I said. But they put you off, they won't tell you anything." The next day when I visited him, he told me, "They're going to collapse the other lung," and a few days after that, "I've sent my resignation in. It's not fair to the club. I won't be ready by September, not at this rate."

It was a watershed, the second, just as the moment in the taxi had been the first. He was admitting, now, that he could no longer control his future.

I went to visit him on the day they'd collapsed his second lung, but at my knock on the door a busy Irish nurse emerged, a tiny red-haired hoyden, shooing me away. "He's not to be seen by *anyone!*" He could not be seen on the second day, nor on the third. When I asked Dr Cowley for news, he responded, with his grin, "Complications. Nothing abnormal. You look after your convalescence, we'll look after him."

Yet still I was not seriously anxious; that great strength, that inflexible will, were sure to see him through. On the fourth day, the nurse popped out and whispered, "You can go in for a minute!" Marshall was lying on his back. His face, tilted to the ceiling, seemed suddenly to have fallen away, his cheeks ravaged from within. "Is it you, Brian?" he asked, in a hoarse, husky voice. "They've really buggered me about."

He stopped then and his eyes closed, but all at once he opened them to say, "Rate I'm going down, I'll be seeking re-election to the sanatorium." But when I asked if there was anything I could get him, he replied, "Nothing, lad, nothing; it's only the after effects."

The days passed, and one's visits were still restricted. His northern friends gathered sombrely in corners, my optimism too brittle and callow for them. "They'll bloody finish him," said Ernie Jacks.

But to me, Marshall was doubly impregnable, impregnable both in himself, and because death, at nineteen, was something which could happen neither to me, nor to my friends. My faith was untroubled even when Marshall's wife arrived, to stay in the village.

We met now and then, sometimes in the sanatorium itself, sometimes while I was on my walks. Her suspicion of me seemed to be diminishing; as we crossed each other at the bridge one afternoon, she said, "You've been good to him. He says you go in every day," and, again, "It's his own fault, he knows it is. Headstrong, he's always the same. He ought never to have gone that day; he'd no business." She was forever bringing him something to eat – chicken, jellies, a Yorkshire pudding – coaxing the appetite which had grown so small.

"You can't even see him now," Ernie Jacks complained, coming gnome-like down the stairs, one evening, as I went up them on my way to visit Marshall. "God knows what they're up to."

It was true; they even had a notice on his door, "No Visitors Without the Permission of Matron".

I took my walks alone, now, thinking of him lying there, alone in the room, of the hollowed face, the mottled hands which looked, resting on the sheet, like the broad skeleton of hands. I would walk very quickly, down the mud-tracks, across the fields, along the sea shore with its dead seaweed and myriad tiny dead starfish, thinking of the stories he'd told me, all of them implicit with his great animal force. The paradox was too huge to reconcile. Soon – after a week, perhaps, a month – the tide would turn, or rather that very force would turn it. He was a footballer and footballers like him were indestructible; I wished I could convey it to his wife, his friends, his mistress.

It was ten days after they had made him incommunicado again that I came out of my chalet, before lunch. It was a clear March morning with a bright sun, and from the hillside, I could see far along the white road which led from the sanatorium to the village. All at once, around the farthest bend, two women came in sight, walking very slowly, side by side. It was almost a minute before I could see that one head was blonde, the other auburn, and it was only then that I knew he was going to die.